"All I want is for someone to trust me," Clay whispered. "To believe me and know what I say is true."

"Oh."

"I'm not sure if I've met her yet or not," he whispered.

"I can't choose you over my brother." Allie felt a moment's anger that he would ask that of her and then she remembered she had been the one to bring up the question about what he wanted.

"I'm sorry," she added.

"So am I," he answered.

He pulled away then and they stood there looking at each other.

She knew without asking that he would not compromise on this point. They were on opposite sides here.

Clay finally moved to open the door and they walked out of the barn.

Sometimes, Allie told herself, a woman had to stick with her family even if her heart wished she could believe something improbable. That was part of being a grown-up. Things did not always go the way one wanted.

Janet Tronstad grew up on her family's farm in central Montana and now lives in Turlock, California, where she is always at work on her next book. She has written more than thirty books, many of them set in the fictitious town of Dry Creek, Montana, where the men spend the winters gathered around the potbellied stove in the hardware store and the women make jelly in the fall.

Visit the Author Profile page
at Harlequin.com for more titles.

Easter in Dry Creek

Janet Tronstad

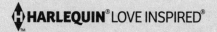

Recycling programs for this product may not exist in your area.

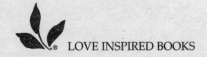

LOVE INSPIRED BOOKS

ISBN-13: 978-0-373-89922-7

Easter in Dry Creek

Copyright © 2017 by Janet Tronstad

www.Harlequin.com

Printed in U.S.A.

And Jesus said, Father, forgive them;
for they know not what they do.
—*Luke* 23:34

This book is dedicated to my new friends
at the Covenant Village of Turlock.
Thanks for the welcome you've given me.

Chapter One

Snowflakes hit his windshield as Clay West peered into the black night, barely managing to see more than a few yards down the icy asphalt road that lay in front of his pickup's headlights. He'd exited the interstate and could see the twenty or so frame buildings that made up the small, isolated town of Dry Creek, Montana. This place—between here and the Nelson ranch—had been the closest thing to a home he'd ever known.

"Not that it worked out," Clay muttered to himself. He'd first come here as a foster kid, and he'd foolishly believed what the social workers said about him finally having a family. Of course, they had been wrong. Being a foster kid wasn't the same as being part of a family.

As he kept the pickup inching forward, Clay

studied the road farther ahead until he gradually realized the town did not look the way he remembered. Four years had passed since he'd lived in this area. He'd been seventeen at the time. The heavily falling snow made it hard to see, especially in the dark, so that might have been part of his confusion now. And maybe it was because of the snowdrifts next to them that the clapboard houses seemed shrunken in the storm. But he didn't recognize the gas station, either.

Suddenly, he asked himself if he'd gone down the wrong road in the night. There were no traffic signs in this part of the state. There hadn't been many turns off the freeway, but he could have chosen the wrong one. Maybe he wasn't where he thought he was. Right then, a gust of wind came out of nowhere. The gray shapes shifted and the town's church materialized out of the swirling storm. "Whoa." He braked to a stop, his fingers gripping the wheel and his breath coming hard. He wasn't as indifferent to this place as he had thought.

The large white building had no steeple. Cement steps led up to an ordinary double door made out of wood. On the ground, a plastic tarp had been laid over flower beds that went along both sides of the church.

One thing was certain, though—he was

looking at the Dry Creek church and none other. Every year the congregation here forced daffodils to bloom for their sunrise Easter service as a sign of their faith.

Clay let the pickup idle for a bit and took a few deep breaths. He wasn't going to be hurried through this town, especially not by his own bad memories. Just then a light was turned on in one of the houses down the road. He tensed for a bit and then shrugged. He told himself that whoever it was would go back to bed. He didn't need to worry. Clay might not be welcome within a hundred miles of here, but he had every legal right to be where he was. The paper in his pocket made that clear when it stated the terms of the early parole he would earn if he spent the next year working as a horse wrangler on the Nelson ranch.

The storm lessened as Clay kept going along the snow-packed road. Finally he came to the drive that led to the heart of the Nelson ranch. When he'd lived here, a locked metal gate always spanned the road just behind the cattle guard. The gate swung free now. Snow had filled in the ditches at the side of the road, but the height of the dead stalks told him that no one had cut back the weeds last fall.

Clay let the pickup sit as he took more time to look around. It was hard to maintain his upbeat attitude looking at the place. He saw a dim light coming from what would be the kitchen of the distant house, but the upstairs was dark. Old habits die hard, and he couldn't help but count across the line of second-floor windows until he found the one that marked Allie Nelson's former room. She was the rancher's daughter. Back before all of his troubles, Clay used to check that window every night from his place in the bunkhouse to see if she had gone to sleep. He never questioned why he did it, but it made him rest easier to know she was safe.

The first portrait sketch Clay had ever drawn was of Allie's young face looking out that window at night, her whole being showing a yearning that touched him in its simplicity. Looking back, he should have known drawing her had been a mistake. She was the one who had made him yearn for some of those promised family ties the social workers told him about.

As Clay pulled closer to the barn, he saw that it wasn't just the weeds that had been neglected. Several poles in the corral were down. He realized then that the windows in the bunkhouse looked deserted. They'd built that log structure the year before he'd been sent here. It was long, with two big main rooms and a porch along the length of it. If there were any ranch hands around, they would have been up stirring by now.

He looked out at the fields then. There used to be dozens of horses standing or galloping around the dirt track that lined the small field to the right. The Nelson ranch supplied stock to other ranches and even managed to sell a few to small racing stables. He and Allie both loved discovering which horses had the strength and speed to be racers. It's what bound them together. Now he saw no animals of any kind.

"Something's wrong," Clay said to himself as he kept looking around.

A light flickered and a woman stepped in front of one of the kitchen windows. Clay could see only her shape, but something about the tilt of her head made him think that it was Allie. His breath stopped at the thought. She'd been a girl of sixteen when he knew her. She had to be twenty years old now. Maybe even twenty-one since her birthday would have been last month. But it couldn't be her; he'd heard she was working at some fancy resort down in Jackson Hole, Wyoming.

He'd rather come up against a dozen raging blizzards than face Allie again. The fierce anger in her eyes at his trial had been harder to bear than hearing the judge pronounce him guilty of armed robbery. He might have endured the censure of the rest of the town if she had stood by him.

He'd been clueless that night about what Allie's older brother, Mark, was capable of doing when he was drunk, but no one believed Clay's version of what happened, especially not Allie. Everyone thought Clay had planned the robbery of the gas station, but it had been Mark's impulsive move.

Clay closed his eyes until the rush of memories stopped. He didn't like thinking about Mark. Allie's brother had been shot in the head that night in a scuffle with the store clerk. At first, everyone expected Mark to come out of his coma in time to testify, but it hadn't happened. The last Clay had heard was that the doctors were saying Mark was not expected to ever regain consciousness. He'd had some kind of fever that compounded the swelling in his brain.

Clay turned the engine off. The pickup jerked as the muffler rattled to a stop. He heard a cat's indignant hiss then and he looked down. He'd forgotten about his passenger. A starving cat had snuck into the pickup when Clay stopped for gas a few hours ago. She was too tame to be feral, but none too friendly, either.

He figured that big empty-looking barn over there might as well house the cat and the kittens that, if he was any judge, she'd be having soon. From the looks of the place, the ranch could use a good mouser. So Clay grabbed the tabby and, without giving her time to protest, tucked her under the coat he was wearing. Someone had left the sheepskin coat on the seat of the pickup that had been left for him in the prison parking lot.

Clay briefly wondered who his benefactor was as he opened the pickup door, stepped down and started walking. Then he told himself he was making too much of the kindness. He was a man who stood alone. That was unlikely to change here.

Inside the house, a thin trail of steam was still rising from the skillet that Allie Nelson had dropped into the sink water before she stepped over to push open the only window that wasn't painted shut in her father's cluttered kitchen. She'd spent the past couple of years working as a fry cook in a popular restaurant in Jackson Hole and, even with that, she had burned the eggs on her first morning back on the ranch.

She'd been in the hall tying her nephew's shoes, but that would be no excuse in her father's eyes. Despite her shouldering the loan payments for her brother's medical bills, which had taken everything she and her father had and which led to her father borrowing against the ranch to pay the rest, her father still treated her like she was barely older than young Jeremy.

The smoke from the skillet was disappearing. The winter air blew in through the open window, and Allie closed her eyes before leaning forward against the counter. She was tired to the bone, she thought as she stood there. But she couldn't give up. The next trip here to the ranch she was going to make sure all of the windows opened as they should. Then she'd get down some of those leftover building supplies from the hayloft in the barn and paint the kitchen walls a bright sunny yellow. She would not like Mark to see the house like this; it was depressing. She'd make their house look happy again before he came home.

Against all odds, her brother had started to slowly come out of his coma this past fall. For a long time the doctors said they expected him to recover. But, when he didn't, they decided things were worse in his brain than they had initially thought. However, Allie's father kept saying Mark had an IQ of 156 and that his son's genius brain would find a way to heal itself.

Allie had heard that IQ statistic so many times growing up that she figured it was seared on her memory. But she did not share her father's confidence in her brother's high IQ to heal him. She turned to someone more powerful. More than once she knelt at her mother's grave and pleaded with God to save her brother, promising she would take better care of him this time if she could only have one more chance.

Now Mark was coming out of his coma. The doctors couldn't explain it. They said it was impossible, but the swelling in his brain had gone down. First, a finger moved, and then some weeks later Mark cleared his throat and tried to speak. Finally, his eyes flickered and he started to eat through a straw. That had gone on for months. Everyone had kept Mark's progress quiet, though. In the beginning, his improvements were so slight that they weren't sure he'd stay on track with his recovery. Then they weren't sure he could take the excitement of other people knowing what had happened.

Allie had gotten back to the ranch only last night, but she was planning to drive to the hospital nursing home to see her brother on Monday.

"You making bacon with them eggs?" Her father's querulous voice floated down the hallway and interrupted her thoughts. "Jeremy and I like bacon with our eggs. Three slices for me."

She looked up but saw no one. Her nephew and her father were still in the back bedroom.

Allie turned to face the hallway. She heard the giggle of her three-year-old nephew and the creak of the springs on her father's bed, which meant that the little boy no doubt raced his plastic horse across the edge of his grandfather's mattress.

Jeremy was bringing joy to this old house, even if they saw him only once in a while. He and his mother lived in Idaho, and this was the first time that she had left Jeremy here alone. Allie had asked for time off from work so she could be here to help watch over him.

"The doctor said you can't have more than a small slice of bacon," Allie called to her father. She'd spoken on the phone with the doctor last week. "Your cholesterol is too high."

Actually, the specialist had said her father should have an aspirin every morning and start eating turkey bacon, but Allie was taking things slowly. Her father refused to consider eating what he called fake bacon. She was stretching the doctor's advice by giving him a small piece of the real stuff and two eggs.

It wasn't until she started back to the sink and passed the smaller window in the kitchen that she glanced out toward the barn and stopped midstride. She hadn't seen that pickup sitting there when she had arrived late yesterday. The pickup was usually parked behind the barn. She didn't know why her father kept the old thing after what happened with it that awful night when Mark had been shot. The pickup was practically falling apart, the red paint faded to mauve except on the dented bumper where the bare metal showed through in a long scratch.

She twisted her neck to get a full view of the yard. Sure enough, a man was walking toward the house.

"Company coming," Allie called as she stood back. Her father must have lent the vehicle to a neighbor and the man was bringing it back. "Best get your robe on."

She picked up the long metal spatula that was lying on the counter. Whoever the man was he had most likely eaten breakfast already, but she didn't want to turn anyone away without some hospitality. Having company in this house was as rare as a party these days. She'd toast slices of the whole-grain bread she'd brought with her from Jackson Hole and pull down the crock of honey to go with it. The coffee was already brewing. She'd also get started on new eggs. Her father would want some even if the other man didn't.

She was pleased to know one of the neighbors had felt free to ask her father for the loan of his old pickup. Ever since Mark had been hurt, her father had stopped going to church services. He said it was because he had to rush to make it to the nursing home before visiting hours closed, but she knew, even though Clay West was clearly the one at fault, her father felt the whole family had been shamed that night. He'd been avoiding everyone since then. He had plenty of time to visit Mark after church.

Allie heard a sound and turned.

"Who is it?" her father asked. He was peeking out a door off the hallway. "I hope it's not Mrs. Hargrove. I'm not presentable. She said she might come by."

Allie would rather the visitor be the sweet older woman. She was the traditional Sunday school teacher for children of Jeremy's age, and Allie thought it was time her nephew joined the class, at least when he was staying with her and her father.

"It looks like a man, so your robe will be fine."

"Does he have on an old sheepskin coat?"

"How'd you know?" she asked as she twirled to stare. Those coats were no longer common. Everyone preferred puffy jackets in neon or pastel colors. For one thing, they were washable, and there wasn't a dry cleaner this side of Miles City.

"I'll put my overalls on." Her father turned without answering her. "I sent Jeremy to his room to get dressed."

Allie stepped over and opened the main door. No one had taken its screen off last fall, and the latch had gotten damp and rusted even more. There were enough things that needed doing in this old house that she could spend a month here instead of the two weeks she'd arranged to take off from her job.

Flakes of snow blew toward the house, sticking to the screen door, but she made no move to wipe them off. Allie shivered from the cold, and her breath was coming out in white puffs. It was difficult to identify the man walking toward the house because he had his head down. The leather coat flapped around his legs. The garment was half-open, and a gray plaid shirt covered his chest. He held one of his arms like he was holding something inside his coat. Worn denim jeans fit his long legs, and cowboy boots sank into the snow.

The morning was overcast, and a burst of wind blew the snow around. The man lifted his face, and suddenly a glimmer of sun came out.

Allie couldn't believe her eyes. It was like her thoughts had conjured up her worst nightmare.

"Clay?" she whispered even though no one could hear her.

His shoulders were broader than she remembered, but she'd recognize his stride anywhere. He was always prepared to take on the world, and it showed in the way he moved. Confident to the point of arrogance. He reminded her of her father in that way.

Clay's dark Stetson left his face in shadows. She couldn't see his black hair or his piercing blue eyes, but it was him all right.

He suddenly stopped midway to the house and stared at the open door. Surely the darkness in the house meant he wouldn't be able to see her clearly enough to know who she was. But he stared as though he could see through the screen and recognize her. He'd always been able to make her feel that he could look right down to her soul. It was those eyes of his.

Of course, that was nonsense, she told herself as she stepped back then, and instinctively slammed the door closed. He had ordinary eyes even if they were a startling icy blue.

"What're you doing that for?" her father asked, grumbling as he limped across the kitchen floor in his slippers. "We got company."

"It's Clay West," Allie said, leaning back against the door.

"Well, so what?" her father asked, his chin up like he was ready to argue. He held a rolled-up magazine in his hand.

"Clay West," she repeated. "You remember—he's the foster kid who lived here. He's the reason Mark is where he is today."

"You don't need to tell me who he is," her father said. "I was here."

"I was, too," Allie protested. She still remembered the night the sheriff had come to their door after midnight. Mark was already in an ambulance on the way to the hospital. Clay sat in the back of the sheriff's car, handcuffed and silent. He never looked up at her.

The sheriff told Allie her brother had been drunk on tequila, but she assured the officer that Mark had never taken a drink of hard liquor in his life. She would know if he had, she'd explained. She was a year younger than Mark, but she'd always been more responsible than he was. As her mother lay dying, she had asked Allie to watch over Mark and make sure he didn't start drinking alcohol. The family was unusually susceptible, she'd said. Mark might have gotten the beer that night, but the empty tequila bottle found in the pickup had to belong to Clay. Allie didn't know why Clay's alcohol blood level wasn't that high, but she knew that the tequila had to belong to him.

Allie's father reached for the door handle. "Clay's probably hungry. He'll want some bacon with his eggs. He's my new ranch hand. And they say he's an artist—sort of like Charlie Russell."

Her father waved the magazine at her.

Allie wondered if her father had started drinking again. He had promised he wouldn't. His fondness for whiskey had nearly ruined their family when she was young. There were no other indications her father had started drinking again, but the possibility had to be examined. She lived too far away to monitor him very well now, but she remembered the past. Alcohol always turned her father's mind fuzzy. He'd get foolish ideas and act on them. And what he said now was preposterous.

"We can't—" She started talking to her father, but he was paying attention only to the man standing outside their door.

Allie had thought she'd never lay eyes on Clay again. It wasn't fair that he walked around every day a whole man while Mark was lying in a convalescent bed staring at the ceiling and struggling to form a coherent sentence.

And now Clay was here—on their porch—and looking better than he had any right to be.

Her world had just turned upside down, and she didn't know what to do about it.

Chapter Two

Clay looked through the screen into the shadows of the kitchen, and his heart sank. For a moment he had thought it was Allie inside the room. Now he saw it was only Mr. Nelson reaching toward the door wearing denim overalls hooked over his white long johns. The unshaven man held a magazine in one hand and fumbled with the catch to open the screen with the other. A lock of his gray hair fell across his brow as he bent his head in concentration. There were lines in the man's face that Clay did not remember being there and dark circles under his eyes.

"Here, let me help you," Clay said as he jiggled the handle on the door from the outside. He had figured out how to make that latch work years ago. A person had to press it just right and it moved smooth as butter.

"You came," the older man said as Clay pushed the door open.

Clay nodded as he stepped into the warmth of the kitchen. It was just as well it was only the two of them. Maybe then the man would tell him why he'd sent for him. When Clay had been convicted of armed robbery, Mr. Nelson told him never to come back to Dry Creek. The old man had meant it that day. People didn't just change their minds for no reason. Maybe the church had put pressure on Mr. Nelson to bring Clay back.

"I can't take your job under false premises—" Clay started, suspecting the rancher would be happy to end this charade, too. He likely hadn't wanted to make the offer in the first place. "So if you plan—"

"Hush," the older man whispered. Then he turned and gave a worried glance at something behind the door. "We can talk later." The man's voice returned to normal. "You'll want breakfast first. Right?"

Before Clay could answer, he heard a feminine gasp.

"Allie?" Clay whispered as he turned to the side. The main part of the kitchen was filled with shadows, but he'd know the sound of her voice anywhere.

In the darkness, he saw her. She stood off

to the side by the refrigerator with a beat-up metal spatula braced in her arms like it was a sword and she was a warrior queen ready to defend her kingdom. She used to love to pretend at games like that. Garden rakes became horses. Leaves made a tiara. She'd told him once that she had wanted to be an actress when she was little. Of course, that was before she fell in love with horses. Then all she wanted was to work on this ranch for the rest of her life.

Clay wished he had a pencil in hand so he could sketch her. A thin glow of morning light was coming through the window, and it outlined her in gold. Her posture showed her outrage and her resolve. She wasn't looking at him, though. Instead, her eyes were fastened on her father.

"I'm not cooking for *him*," she announced as she jabbed the long-handled spatula in Clay's general direction. It was a dismissive gesture. Then she crossed her arms, letting the metal implement stick out.

Well, Clay thought, trying to hide his smile, at least someone in Dry Creek believed in telling the truth as she saw it. He should be upset, but he couldn't take his gaze off Allie. She'd always fascinated him. Gradually, however, as he studied her, he realized the young teen he'd known was all grown up. The girlish lines of her face were gone, and she had the sleekness of a sophisticated young woman even in the faded apron she wore tied around her denim jeans. Her auburn hair was thick and as unruly as he remembered, although she'd tried to pull it into some order and knot it at the back of her neck. The pink in her cheeks was no doubt due to the cold that had come in from the opened door, but it made her look impassioned.

"I don't need to eat." Clay spoke mildly, and then he swallowed. This new Allie made him feel self-conscious. He wished he had taken time to get a haircut before he left the prison. "I do have something to say, however—"

"It'll do no good to say you are sorry," Allie interrupted as she stepped closer and stood in the light of the open door. She gave him a withering look. "Words won't make one bit of difference to Mark. And you should close the door."

"Sorry," Clay said as he reached behind him and did so. "But I wasn't going to apologize."

No one answered, and the tension in the room jumped higher. Clay figured a new haircut wouldn't have made him look much better.

"Now, Allie," Mr. Nelson finally said. "Clay's a guest in this house. And, of course, he's going to eat. Your mother wouldn't send anyone away hungry. You know that."

Allie turned to Clay, and he felt the air leave his lungs. She'd changed again. The sprinkling of freckles across her nose was the same, but her green eyes blazed. They showed the same fury that had consumed her at the trial. He had hoped the years would have softened her toward him.

"I'll make you some toast and you can be on your way," she finally said.

"I have no quarrel with you," he answered quietly. He missed the girl who had been his friend. "Never did."

"Nobody here is quarreling," Mr. Nelson said firmly as he frowned at Allie. "We know how to be civil."

Clay snuck another peak at Allie. The fire was gone from her eyes, but he did not like the bleakness that replaced it.

"I just want to explain," Clay said then. There was so much he wanted to say to Allie, and this might be his only chance to say anything. But he had to be wise.

"You okay these days?" he asked.

She didn't even blink.

He figured that all he could speak of was that night. "I should have convinced Mark to go back to the ranch earlier that night. But the robbery—it wasn't my doing. That bottle of te-quila wasn't mine. I didn't know Mark had it with him. I was driving. It was dark inside the cab of the pickup. I thought he was still drinking his bottle of beer. We each had one. And I was pumping fuel into the pickup when he took the rifle off the rack behind us and went into the gas station. I didn't even see him at first. I had no idea what he planned."

"Are you saying Mark was the one at fault?" The fire in her eyes came back. Her voice was clipped as she faced Clay squarely. "That you didn't know anything about it?"

"I'm not saying he was at fault—" Clay stopped, unsure how to proceed. He didn't need an apology for the way anyone had treated him. He didn't want her to think that. He wanted her to believe him because she trusted him to tell the truth. Her opinion of him mattered, and he'd fight for it.

"It's cowardly to blame Mark when he can't even defend himself," she said, her voice low and intense. "I know Mark, and I know he wouldn't plan any robbery. It had to be you. I thought all those years in prison would have taught you to tell the truth if nothing else."

Clay studied Allie's face. She was barely holding on to her tears. He knew how that felt.

"I already knew how to tell the truth," he

said softly. "I had barely stepped inside the place when the rifle went off. Mark and the station clerk were already struggling with each other when I saw them—I told everyone that at the trial. That's why all they could charge me with was being an accessory to the crime."

Clay saw the battle inside Allie. She never liked fighting with anyone, but he could see she was determined to blast him away from here. At least her anger seemed to have pushed back her tears. He could take the hit if it made her feel better.

"You were judged guilty," she said firmly. Her eyes flashed. "Everyone agreed. I don't understand how you can stand there and pretend to be innocent."

"I have no choice." Clay hoped his face didn't show his defeat. The two of them would never be friends again. Maybe they never had been. "I have to stand here and tell you what happened if I want you to know the truth. I'm sorry if you can't accept it."

Mr. Nelson cleared his throat as though he was going to speak. Clay held up his hand and looked at the older man. "I know my parole is tied to this job. If it doesn't work out, you can call someone and they will contact the local sheriff—I'm assuming Carl Wall is the one here. Anyway, since the pickup is yours, I have to leave it here. The sheriff will see that I get back to prison. Thanks, too, for having the vehicle sent over. You can decide."

Mr. Nelson was silent.

"You just got here," the rancher finally mumbled, looking uncomfortable.

Clay nodded. He still wasn't sure why he'd been asked to come, but he wasn't going to stay if it was a problem. He'd learned his lesson about making sure he was wanted before he stayed anyplace.

"Everybody knows—" Allie started to say. She stopped when Clay looked at her.

"Everybody doesn't know as much as they think they do," he finally said.

She didn't answer. It was so quiet in the kitchen that Clay thought he could hear the cat inside his coat purring. The heater in the pickup he'd driven over hadn't worked very well, and the tabby was likely content just to be out of the cold. Clay sometimes wished he could be satisfied with the small victories in life like that. A good dinner. A moment's comfort. They should be enough. Instead, he wanted people, especially Allie, to know who he was. And no one could claim to know Clay West if they thought he was a liar. He probably shouldn't care, but he did.

"Do they still ask people in the church to

stand up and say what's wrong in their lives?" he asked. That was the only way he knew to address everyone in the area. He wouldn't need to stay for the sermon.

"You mean for prayers?" Allie sounded surprised. Then her eyes slid over him suspiciously. "You want to ask *us* to pray for you?"

"The church will be happy to pray for you," Mr. Nelson said as he waved the magazine in the air. "Everyone has read about you here. The hardware store got in a dozen copies. The ranchers are all talking about you as they sit around that stove in the middle of the store. You remember that stove? You're practically famous there."

Clay felt a sudden desire to sit down, but he couldn't. Not yet.

He never should have done that interview for the *Montana Artist Journal*. Allie was looking at him skeptically.

"That reporter exaggerated," Clay said. "I'm no Charlie Russell in the making—except for maybe that we both like to roam. I sketch faces and scenes. Simple pencil drawings. That's all." He'd had offers from a couple of magazines to print his prison sketches and had even gotten an art agent out of the deal, but Clay saw no reason to mention that. "And I'm not interested in anyone praying for me. I just want to set the record straight on what happened that night with Mark. I want the facts known."

One of the few things Clay remembered from his early life was his father urging him to always tell the truth. Both his parents had died soon after that in a car accident. Clay clung to that piece of advice because it was all he had left of his family. He wanted to feel that he belonged to them no matter where he went.

Allie looked at him. "I won't have you saying bad things about Mark."

Clay studied her. She no longer seemed to be as angry, but she was wary.

"I'll just tell what happened." Clay paused before continuing. "That's all I'm aiming for. And, after that, if you still don't want me here, I will go back. I can't make people believe me. I didn't have high hopes coming here anyway. I can even stay somewhere else tonight. Tomorrow's Sunday, right? Does Mrs. Hargrove still rent out that room above her garage?"

The older woman had been the only one to stand up for him at his trial, and he counted her as a friend. She had sent him cards every birthday and Christmas while he had been locked up. He'd done his best to send her cards in return. Usually he enclosed a few sketches; over time he'd sent her a dozen Dry Creek scenes. The café. The hardware store. Every

main building, except for the church. He'd
never managed a sketch of that. He wouldn't
mind spending a couple of nights in her rental
room before he headed back to prison. He had
sold enough pencil portraits to other prisoners
over the years to have a tidy sum in a savings
account. He could pay for the room easily.

"Mrs. Hargrove?" Allie asked, frowning.
"I'm sure the parole board doesn't want you
speaking out and giving good people like her
a hard time. She's having trouble with her feet
these days."

"The parole board sent me here." Clay felt
guilty that he hadn't known about the aches
in the older woman's feet. "They had to figure
I'd talk to someone. Besides, I can even help
Mrs. Hargrove out some if I'm at her place.
It could be a good thing. She probably needs
logs for that woodstove of hers. The winter
is going on long this year. I could get her all
set with more firewood. Some kindling, too.
She'd like that."

"The board probably doesn't realize the
harm you could do here." Allie turned to face
her father again, and Clay couldn't see her expression. "But we know."

Mr. Nelson cleared his throat, eyeing his
daughter. "Don't look at me that way. We're
not sending him away."

"Why not?" Clay asked softly. Father and daughter both turned to him in concern. He had to admit he was a little taken aback himself, but nothing was ever gained by dodging the truth. He spoke to Mr. Nelson. "When I saw you last, you were determined to make me suffer for what happened. I remember what you said. 'Let him rot in that black hole of a place. We don't want him back here.' So I'm asking straight out, what's changed?"

The rancher paled at Clay's words. "I suppose you want an apology from me, too, now?"

Clay shook his head impatiently. "I just want a plainspoken answer. Why am I here?"

Mr. Nelson stood there thinking for a minute.

"For what it's worth, I am sorry," the older man finally said. "I said awful things to you and about you. No Christian should say such things."

"People say a lot of things they shouldn't," Clay said. "Christian or not."

Allie started to say something, but her father held up a hand to stop her. "He has a right to ask what's going on."

Everyone was silent. Clay watched as the older man debated something.

"I'm doing this for Mark," Mr. Nelson finally admitted, his voice thick with emotion.

The rancher continued speaking, his eyes on Clay. "I didn't want to ask you, but I finally realized we need you. There's no one else."

Clay saw defeat in the other man's eyes. Clay had been in prison long enough to recognize the look on a man's face when he had no choice except the bitter one in front of him. The man was finally being honest.

"But you still blame me?" Clay asked. He wanted things to be clear.

The older man didn't answer.

"Will you help us anyway?" Mr. Nelson finally asked.

"I don't see how I—" Clay began to politely refuse the request. There were worse things than being locked up in a cell. Being around people who didn't trust him was one of them. He'd be free on his own terms in two years. He could wait.

Allie had been silent, but now she sputtered indignantly a moment until she found words. "Mark would be the last person to want *him* here to help."

Anger scorched the air.

Clay tried not to wince. "I should leave."

He decided he'd call Sheriff Wall himself if he had to. If it warmed up outside, he could hitchhike back to prison. He had more sketches to do there anyway.

Clay waited for Allie to turn around, but she kept facing her father with her back stiff enough to make her displeasure clear.

"Please don't look at me that way," Mr. Nelson said to her. "We have no choice. Mark wants to see Clay. Mark has always looked on him as a brother."

Allie jerked sideways. She could barely believe her ears. "What?"

Allie turned to look, and Clay seemed as stunned as she was. His eyes were wide and his jaw slack.

"They're not brothers," Allie swiveled and told her father crisply, ignoring Clay's question. She needed to put a stop to this nonsense. She hadn't been to see Mark for several months, but she hadn't heard him mention Clay before that. Of course, it was only recently that her brother was able to speak very complicated thoughts. And her father said Mark had improved since she'd seen him last.

Finally, she turned back to Clay. "Sorry, but that's the way it is. I don't know what went on between the two of you, but a brother doesn't do their brother harm."

Clay smiled grimly. "Believe me, I wish I'd tried to stop things. But I didn't know what he was planning to do that night. I certainly never meant for him to end up like he did. I worry about him just like you do."

Allie had watched Clay as he spoke. He wasn't lying. It didn't mean he was telling the complete truth, though. Maybe that was the way he thought it had happened, she told herself. He could have set everything in motion and then wished later that he had pulled back.

"I know you didn't mean for Mark to end up in a coma." Allie could give him that much. And she knew Mark liked Clay; her brother had spent many of his evenings out in the bunkhouse since that was where Clay slept. They'd sit at one of the tables and play checkers. Their father hadn't liked it, but no one had stopped it.

Allie supposed it was money that had prompted Clay to plan that robbery. She had always thought that when he turned eighteen, he'd just stay on as a regular ranch hand. But maybe he was worried about his future. Then again maybe all he wanted was more beer to drink and he hadn't known how else to get it.

Clay hadn't responded to her, and she looked up at him. *Lord, what do I do?* she prayed.

Her father was right. She needed to be kinder to Clay. She wished she had known he needed more money; she could have turned over her allowance. After all, he hadn't had the advantage of having parents to raise him as she had. If the parole board was sending him back to where the crime had been committed, they must have their reasons.

Clay met her eyes, but his expression didn't soften. He certainly didn't act like someone who needed her charity.

"I still don't see what I can do for Mark, though," Clay finally said. She could hear the skepticism in his voice as he eyed her father. "I'm not a doctor. I don't know what to do about a coma. I don't believe in miracles, and I don't pray. God would never grant a request from me. I'm not a faith healer. There's not one thing I can do but say I am sorry that Mark is hurting."

Allie couldn't believe he was not going to at least pretend to help them. Not when it meant he'd be out of prison. She remembered now how stubborn he'd always been.

In the silence, her father spoke to her. "Mark told me a few weeks ago that he asked Clay to help him with the Easter sunrise processional."

She heard Clay gasp, but she focused on her father. He spoke slowly and deliberately, like he wanted a certain response from her. "You remember how Mark had been talking to everyone about that processional before the accident?"

"I do," Allie acknowledged as she reached over and put a hand on her father's arm. The poor man had aged two decades in the last four years. She was concerned about him. He carried a burden that never seemed to leave him. At least she was distracted from their family problems by working long shifts at her job.

"I doubt Mark means for you to worry," she said to her father.

"That's what he says," her father agreed. "And I know he doesn't know so much time has passed."

"I can't believe Mark is communicating," Clay said.

Allie suddenly realized that Clay still had that sheepskin coat wrapped around him. It had been cold outside, and she wasn't sure the heater in that old pickup worked very well. He must have been frozen when he stepped inside the kitchen.

When her father didn't answer, Clay turned toward her.

Allie nodded. Clay's eyes widened.

"So what, does he blink his eyes at you?" Clay asked her. "You know, the old 'once for yes and twice for no' kind of a thing?" He kept looking at her, but she gestured to her father, suggesting he was the one to answer. Clay turned to him. "I've heard of things like that—people pointing to letters in the alphabet. Is that the kind of thing Mark is doing?"

"Oh, no," her father said as he shook his head. "Nothing like that."

Allie could see the excitement leave Clay's face again. He was disappointed.

"Then what is it?" Clay asked.

No one answered. Allie wasn't sure what kind of a deal the prison officials had made with her father, but it would have to be canceled. They didn't need someone around asking probing questions about Mark. Besides, she couldn't afford to pay a ranch hand. And, there was no need for one anyway. The corrals and barn were empty. There were enough repairs to keep a man busy for months, but that work would have to wait.

"We don't talk much about Mark," her father finally said. "The doctors say to keep it quiet."

"You're going to have to tell me," Clay said then, his voice insistent. "You brought me all the way over here. And I'm not going anywhere until I understand what's going on with Mark."

Allie could have told her father that this would happen. But they couldn't protect Mark if they told everyone all there was to know about his condition.

Clay looked at her.

"My father knows more about it than I do," Allie said. She'd leave it up to him to walk through this minefield.

"But you can tell him better than me," her father protested, looking over at her in alarm.

She shook her head. She wasn't the one who had invited Clay here; it was her father. She was tired of being the one who handled the problems in the family, especially when they were not of her making. She should go check on Jeremy anyway. She had heard the closet door open in the far bedroom some time ago. The boy was likely back there playing with those plastic horses of his. It wouldn't hurt if she stayed out here a bit, though, and saw how much her father was willing to share with Clay.

"One of you better tell me," Clay said.

He looked at her, pale blue eyes searching hers for answers. He wasn't afraid to push for what he wanted to know. A muscle along his jaw tightened, and she knew he'd not be discouraged.

"It's not my place to say," she finally managed to tell him.

She wondered if Clay had any idea how complicated life had become in the Nelson family since the day of that attempted robbery. There were many times since then when she wished Clay was still around so she could talk to him about the problems she had. He'd always seemed so steady in his advice. The truth was that she had relied on him more than Mark and certainly more than her father. Her brother had refused to acknowledge any issues in their family. Her father, when he was drinking, had been no help as he had often been the source of her concern.

After her mother died, Allie felt like she was the one in charge of keeping the family together. So far, she hadn't done very well.

Allie didn't like being on the spot again, because one look at Clay's eyes and she knew he wouldn't be satisfied with some half-truth that she would tell him, hoping to satisfy his questions.

"Don't worry about it," Clay said to her softly then. "Your father will tell me."

Allie could only hope that would be true.

Chapter Three

The kitchen was gaining light, Clay noticed
as he stood there in the silent room. The clock
read seven o'clock. The room looked like it
hadn't been touched since he left here four
years ago. The same beige paint was on the
walls, and the windowsills were a chipped
white. He had noticed a nail by the refrigerator. It held last year's calendar, and it didn't
appear like the months on it had even been
changed.

"Tell me about Mark," Clay finally asked
again as he turned his attention to the older
man. "If he doesn't make some hand motions,
how does it work?"

Clay figured the rancher must be imagin-
ing some kind of response from his son. The
signs of depression were all over this kitchen.
Even in prison, the officials became concerned

when something as simple as a calendar wasn't kept updated. Clay guessed Mr. Nelson was telling himself he knew what Mark thought. It was like people who decided their cat was an opera fan because the animal sat there and purred when a song was being sung. He supposed it was very human to imagine that one could know the thoughts of a being who couldn't communicate.

Mr. Nelson didn't say anything. Allie, on the other hand, was standing there with a blank look on her face that was so uncharacteristic of her that Clay suspected she was unwilling to tip anyone off to her father's strange beliefs. Maybe she was embarrassed.

"I know it's been hard," Clay said, trying not to let his disappointment show. He might be having those flights of fancy, too, if he was father to someone in a coma. But desperate hope could mess with a man's mind; no one knew that better than men who had spent time behind bars.

"Oh, no, Mark is talking," Mr. Nelson said with strength in his voice. He seemed to have understood what Clay was thinking. "It's not easy. He has to come up with the words, and it's slow. But he's talking."

"He says actual words?"

Mr. Nelson nodded. "More now than when he started."

Clay looked at the man for a long moment. Then he turned to Allie. She nodded, as well. It was a wooden nod, like something was holding her back, but she did confirm the words.

"He used to just make sounds and we had to guess at the words," Allie offered.

Clay felt joy start to blossom inside him. "Well, what do you know?" Clay said as he lifted his fist in a gesture of triumph. Mark—his friend, his buddy—was free from the blackness of being in a coma. He'd heard enough stories from men who had spent the night in solitary confinement to have some sense of what that release must feel like to Mark. Not to mention the hope it would bring to his family.

Clay had a sudden impulse to wrap his arms around Allie and coax her into dancing an Irish jig with him. They'd done that once in the rain when they'd clocked a good time racing some of the horses. He, Mark and Allie, all dancing in a circle in the barn and laughing like fools. He needed to do something to celebrate. But he said nothing because he saw Allie was blinking back tears.

"What's wrong?" Clay asked anxiously. "Am I missing something?"

He supposed Mark could be talking and dying at the same time. That would explain the pinched look on Allie's face.

She shook her head. "Oh, no. These are happy tears."

Clay never had understood those kinds of tears. But he was glad Mark was apparently all right.

Suddenly Clay could feel the cat stirring. He put his hand over the place where the feline struggled against the coat, hoping to calm her until he could get her out from inside it.

Then he heard a sound and glanced down in time to see a movement out of the corner of one eye. A young boy was sneaking into the kitchen from the hallway. His flannel pajamas had pictures of galloping horses on them. His dark hair had a cowlick on the left side and was not combed.

The cat seemed to be calm now. Clay relaxed.

The boy slid forward and stood beside Allie. She put her hand on his head without even seeming to realize he was there. Then she stroked his hair in absentminded affection.

"I couldn't find my clothes." The boy looked up. "I want the blue shirt."

"So you've been playing instead of getting dressed like Grandpa asked," Allie said with strong affection in her voice as she leaned down to kiss the top of the boy's head. The boy nodded sheepishly. Then Allie straightened up.

Clay had never imagined that Allie would have a son. But just because time had stood still for him during the past several years, it didn't mean it had slowed for anyone else.

He knew Allie well enough to realize that if she had a son it also meant she likely had a husband. He supposed he'd never had a real chance with her, but it still left him empty. He'd pictured her so many times when he was in prison; there was something about her that reminded him of fireflies. Delicate yet bright, flitting from place to place. She always lifted his spirits. He would have given anything to be able to date her. Maybe give her a first kiss.

Clay must have shifted his shoulders as he stood there staring because the cat twisted inside his coat again. He saw that she'd pulled at one of the buttons until it was open. Before Clay could reach down and grab the animal, she flew through the air, landing on her feet atop the worn beige linoleum floor.

"What's that?" Mr. Nelson demanded to know. He looked around like more cats might be flying toward him from everywhere.

The tabby, its rust-colored fur bristling,

stood there in the middle of the kitchen arching her back and looking pleased with her flight. Then she hissed. Clay had no doubt the cat was ready to defend herself from any scolding. But the young boy slid down until he was sitting in front of her.

"Don't touch her," Clay cautioned as he bent down and put his hands out to protect the child. "She's partly wild."

The cat had likely been tame at some point, but Clay figured she'd forgotten any softness she'd ever known. It had been a long time since she'd had an owner, and he knew how quickly home manners could be forgotten. The boy was already pulling the cat toward him, though. Once he had her in his arms, he rubbed his face against her matted fur.

The feline looked up suspiciously, but she didn't fight.

"I always wanted a kitty," the boy said and gave a satisfied sigh. "And this one has orange stripes. That's my favorite color. Does that mean she's for me?"

He patted the tabby gently, as though he'd already claimed her.

Clay was glad the boy had never seen a tiger.

"Orange is a good color," Clay agreed, noticing that the cat had relaxed in the boy's care. Maybe she remembered more than he thought.

"It's the color for caution, though, so be careful."

Clay braced himself to make a grab if the cat started to claw her way out of the boy's embrace, but she stayed where she was. "I expect you'll want to ask your father if you can keep her."

Clay knew he shouldn't have asked it that way. But he wanted to know. He tried to keep his expression neutral. Allie looked like someone's wife, with her hair pulled back in a barrette and a faded apron covering her jeans. He hoped that whoever the man was he was decent toward her and the boy.

"We don't talk about his father," Allie told Clay and gave him a warning look. Her eyes darkened to steel as she stood her ground. She continued, speaking to the boy. "You'll have to ask your mother, though."

"Good," Clay whispered. He felt his face smile. So Allie wasn't the boy's mother.

Allie was studying him again now as though she was wondering at his thoughts.

"I—" Clay stammered. He didn't want her to know what he'd been thinking. She saw too much. He could tell by the questions shimmering in her eyes. He'd never been able to hide much from her. "The cat needs a good home."

That wasn't a lie, Clay assured himself. All

those years ago, his father never had said anything about whether one had to always tell the
entire truth.

"Everyone needs a home," Clay added to
give more weight to his earlier words.

The pink on Allie's cheeks flashed red. "Are
you saying we did wrong by you? We gave you
a home as long as we could."

"I just meant the cat," Clay said gently. He
was glad he hadn't made the mistake of thinking the color on her face came from warm
memories of him.

"Oh," Allie said.

Clay turned so he didn't see her. He'd give
her privacy if that's what she wanted. Everyone was silent.

"The kitty has too many bones," the boy finally said as he looked up at Clay.

Allie bent down, obviously relieved to have
a change in the conversation. "The poor thing's
half-starved and is going to deliver a full litter any day now." Allie glared at Clay. "Don't
you feed her?"

"She hitched a ride with me—that's all," he
protested. "Someone abandoned her and no
one would take her in. I did what I could for
her. I bought some packets of coffee creamer
at the gas station and fed her."

"Creamer?" Allie raised her eyebrow in question. "That's not enough."

"It was the middle of the night and I wasn't near any four-star restaurants. It was creamer, candy bars or coffee. Not much choice," Clay said. "And I scooped up a lot of packets."

The owner of the station had charged him plenty for the creamer, too. They'd found a glass ashtray and opened the packets of liquid and poured them into that. The cat had licked up three servings. Clay had to buy the ashtray, too, because the station owner said he couldn't sell it after it had been licked by a cat.

"I think she's still hungry, Auntie," the boy said.

"Speaking of hungry," Mr. Nelson said then, looking more like the man he had been when Clay knew him. "I'm sure we could all eat something." He glanced over at Clay. "How about we have some eggs and bacon to go with that toast?"

Clay nodded. "I'd like that if Allie's willing." He didn't want to press things with her. "Just this once. It was a long, cold drive over here."

"I'm glad you came," Mr. Nelson admitted.

It was quiet until Allie spoke to the boy. "Now, you go take the cat into the back bedroom and get dressed. There are some of your

clothes in the closet hanging on the short bar.
I think the blue shirt is there. Then get some
of those old towels that Grandpa keeps in the
bottom drawer of his dresser. The ones he uses
to shine his Sunday shoes. They'll make a nice
soft bed for the mama cat."

"But," Mr. Nelson protested, "my shoes—"

"I'll get you some other rags," Allie told
her father. "We have plenty of old towels out
in the bunkhouse. I just need to cut them up."

Mr. Nelson shrugged. "Well, okay then."

The little boy eagerly started walking toward the hallway.

Clay felt happy just watching him.

Allie waited until she heard Jeremy open the
door to the back bedroom. Then she turned
to Clay. She saw he had taken his hat off, but
she refused to be distracted by the directness
of his gaze.

"We try not to upset Jeremy," Allie told him.
She hated to have to reveal all their family secrets, but she could see Clay was curious, and
she didn't want him to start asking questions.
"Jeremy's mother has just started letting him
visit here by himself now. We don't want anything to stop that."

Allie watched Clay as he nodded slowly.
The warm kitchen air had returned the color

to his skin, but Allie noticed lines around his eyes that hadn't been there when she used to know him.

"The boy's mother?" Clay asked. "She's a friend of yours?"

Allie blinked. "I never really thought about it. She's more—that is, I only knew Hannah because of Mark. They were both ahead of me in school—you know how it is. She and I didn't know each other really. But she grew up around here, too."

Clay had been her best friend back then. Not that he'd known it. Mark was gone so much, though, with Hannah, and the ranch had been lonely. Clay had actually been a good companion to her because he liked the horses, too. At least, she had always thought that was why they got along so well.

Her father grunted then. "Jeremy's mother is Mark's old girlfriend. The only one he's ever had."

Allie saw the truth dawning in Clay's eyes.

She nodded. "Hannah Stelling."

Clay was silent for a bit before speaking. "Jeremy is Mark's son?"

Allie nodded.

"Does he know?" Clay asked.

"We thought Hannah should be the one to tell him," Allie said. "And all she ever says is that Mark broke up with her and that's that. Case closed."

"But she's the one who broke up with him," Clay protested. "And Mark didn't say she was pregnant. I'm sure he would have mentioned that if he had known. He was just mad she had given him an ultimatum—marriage or nothing. That's why we went out that night. My birthday wasn't until the next day, but it was still a good excuse to have a beer and let off some steam."

"There was no good excuse for the two of you to have a beer," Allie said primly. "Neither one of you was of age." She had preached that to her brother until she ran out of breath. She saw now that she should have included Clay in her instructions.

"You got the beer?" her father asked then, more eager than Allie would have expected since he never wanted to talk about where the liquor came from on that night. She always thought he felt guilty for not cautioning them about how strong alcohol could affect them.

Clay shook his head. "Mark had it. He gave me one bottle and kept the other."

"It wasn't just the beer," Allie said, her eyes pointed to Clay. "It was that tequila, and we all know you had to be the one getting that."

"Why do you say that?" Clay asked incredulously.

Allie bristled. She didn't know why he couldn't just admit what he had done. "It's obvious. Mark had no way to get tequila. There wasn't a gas station around here that carried it. I checked. Besides, you have your ways. You probably learned all about how to get liquor when you were a kid in the big city."

It was the same place he'd learned all about girls, she thought. Mark had warned her that Clay thought nothing of kissing girls and so she should be careful around him. Unfortunately, her brother's warning had only made her more fascinated with Clay.

"Because I was a foster kid?" he asked, the edge to his voice making Allie feel a little nervous. "Is that what you mean? That I automatically break the law because I'm a foster kid?"

"It's not just that, but you have to admit—" she began.

"No, I don't," Clay interrupted. "I might have grown up rough, but I never was much on drinking. I never bought any alcohol. I wasn't of age, and I wasn't about to lie when someone asked if I was legal."

Allie paused and forced herself to swallow the accusations she was going to make. Clay had a point. She knew he wouldn't stand there and lie to a clerk in a liquor store. She had always figured that the only reason he had not told the truth about the robbery at his trial was because he didn't want to go to prison. She did not understand why he would not admit it now, though.

"It doesn't matter where the alcohol came from," her father said with enough force to his voice to remind Allie of what was important.

"The real problem was Hannah breaking up with Mark," Clay added. "That's all he could talk about. She asked him to go for a drive at noon and told him it was over unless they got married."

"He should have known Hannah wasn't really breaking up with him," Allie said. "They'd been dating forever. She didn't tell him she was pregnant because she wanted him to marry her for love and not feel like he'd been trapped. But she wasn't leaving him. If you hadn't been there to egg Mark on, he would have eventually come around and seen how things were."

"But she didn't say any of that," Clay protested. "What was he to think?"

"Most men don't think," she said, not expecting the bitterness she heard in her voice. She was disappointed by more than what had happened with Hannah and Mark. Clay had thrown away their chances, too. "That's the problem."

"Now, Allie," her father protested.

She lifted her chin. "Well, it's true. Men do what they want and don't even always tell you what happened. They just let the pieces fall anywhere."

Allie let her words hang in the air. She wasn't going to take them back. She could see Clay measuring her words, like he wasn't sure what she meant. She saw the muscles tighten along his jaw, and she knew he had decided something.

"You're talking about me now, aren't you?" he said, no longer looking puzzled.

She didn't answer. As strong as her memories of him were, she had no right to question him. There had been no hint of romance in his manner toward her that time so long ago. He'd never even tried to kiss her, not even when she had bought tube after tube of lip gloss with enticing names like Sweet Pink and Red Passion. That should show her what Clay thought of her and kissing.

"I don't lie, and I wasn't letting anyone down," Clay finally said. "That night with Mark—no one was counting on me. There was no one to let down."

Yes, there was, Allie thought as she stepped back toward the kitchen sink. *There was me.*

She wasn't ready for all of this. She'd thought she'd never see Clay again. But he was wrong that no one had counted on him back then. Her father had still been drinking his whiskey, bottle after bottle of the same, and she used to tell herself Clay would know what to do if she needed help. Her mother had been the one to handle her father when he was drunk, and once she was gone, Allie never knew how to keep him steady. Mark refused to think there was a problem with their father, and so she knew it would be up to her to do something, if her father went out of control. That's why she'd been glad Clay was with them.

She'd worried all the time back then until one night when she'd seen Clay standing outside the bunkhouse looking up at her window. His gaze had seemed protective, and she told herself he was looking out for her a little bit. She knew he would come if she needed help. That's when she'd started her search for the perfect irresistible lip gloss. She had barely gotten used to the flutter of her feelings for him and then he was gone.

Deep silence filled the room.

Finally Allie turned around and spoke. She

didn't look up, but she knew Clay would understand she was speaking to him. Those long-ago feelings were not important. She needed to help her family now, and she couldn't do that by mooning over Clay. "Hannah only took Jeremy to see Mark once a long time ago. Jeremy was scared of the coma, and so now she leaves him here with Dad when she goes. Jeremy doesn't know who his father is."

"You haven't told the boy?" Clay asked.

Allie shook her head. So many things had been left undone. "He hasn't really asked us. I think Hannah just told him his father was gone. Jeremy seems too young to care much."

"He's not too young," Clay said.

"I suppose not," Allie said. "I've wondered what he thinks about having a grandfather and an aunt, but no father."

"I wish there was something I could do," Clay said.

"Thanks," Allie said. "But in the end, it's not your problem. You're free now and Mark's stuck in that nursing home."

"Now, Allie," her father interrupted her. "Clay did his time in prison."

"Not all of it," Allie said. "He shouldn't be out yet. I've kept track. If the parole board hadn't sent him here, he'd be serving two more years."

She had planned to send him a few hundred dollars just before he was set for release. She hadn't wanted to think he might be hungry. And if it was anonymous, no one had to know.

"I got him paroled early," her father replied.

Allie forgot the mellow kindness she'd been feeling and turned to look at her father in shock. "You did what?"

"It's called victim reparations. I called up the parole board and said we needed help on the ranch. They were reluctant, but I said there was no one here to work since Mark wasn't able and I asked them to send Clay. I didn't want to mention Mark's recovery. I figured it was best to keep it simple."

Allie continued to stare at her father. "Is that legal? You telling them to send him like that?"

She looked at Clay and saw him wince.

"I am okay with it," Clay said. "Especially now that I know about Mark."

"But he's the reason Mark is hurt." Allie stared at her father, willing him to meet her gaze. Everyone was forgetting what was important. "Clay should go back and finish his time. I can't believe you asked them to release him."

She'd been prepared to accept that Clay was sorry if he was getting paroled because the authorities thought he'd done enough time. But if her father had been the one to suggest it, that changed everything. No one else necessarily thought the time was sufficient.

Mr. Nelson kept looking at the floor. "What was I supposed to do? Mark was asking for Clay. Besides, I need help with the ranch. It's falling apart."

She could see the condition of the ranch for herself. Each month she put what she could into a small savings account so she could save enough for some barn repairs.

"We'll fix things up around here later," Allie whispered fiercely. "We've got time."

"No, we don't," her father said, and he gave a proud grin. Her mother used to call that her father's Cheshire cat face. It meant he had done something no one would expect. And, usually, something her mother wouldn't have approved.

Allie had a bad feeling about this. "What do you mean?"

"I bought some more horses," her father announced. "Real cheap from a rancher over by Bozeman."

"You bought—" Allie gasped. She wasn't sure she had heard him right. "We can't afford anything. Nothing. You know that. Maybe some chickens."

Her father snorted. "We need more than

chickens to turn this place around. Some prime horseflesh is what will put us back in business."

"You bought purebred stock?" Allie asked. She didn't even want to know how much that would cost. They had already squeezed the budget as tight as they could. The reason she wanted to start taking some accounting classes was to help with the ranch records. When Mark had received that scholarship and declared he wanted to be a doctor, she had felt free to stake her claim to the ranch. The horses themselves had lots of details that needed tracking. They'd need to buy more animals eventually, but not yet.

"The bank lent me enough to pay for them," her father said, a note of satisfaction coming into his voice. "I don't want Mark to come home and see the corrals empty like they are. We need some horses. They're being delivered any day now. I'm not quite sure on the time."

Allie stared at him. She couldn't breathe thinking about more debt. She could barely pay back what they had now.

"They're good horses," her father repeated himself, the dreamy look on his face telling her that he was lost in his own world. "The best bloodlines we can find. It's a deal. Four horses, three of them mares all set to have colts this spring. One of them is lame, but the sire, who is coming, too, is almost a purebred. At least that's what I heard. And one of the colts could be a racer. The others might go for range horses when they've had a chance to fill out. All of them for five hundred dollars."

She heard Clay grunt in astonishment, but he didn't speak.

"That can't be right," Allie finally managed to say. Her head was spinning. "That's way too low. Are the animals sick? Or was it five thousand dollars? Even that's not enough for that many good horses. Maybe you've got the numbers wrong. That happens, you know, when you've been—"

Allie stopped. She gave a quick glance over at Clay. This was private family business. She looked back at her father. "You know."

"I haven't been drinking," her father protested, sounding offended. "The man who sold them to me owed me a favor from way back. He's giving me a special deal."

"You're sure?" Allie's voice sounded distant to her own ears. It took a sharp woman to outwit a drunk. She'd searched the kitchen cupboards for alcohol and hadn't found anything. She always did that first thing when she got home.

"Of course I'm sure." Her father glared at

her. "I'm going to go back and check on Jeremy."

Her father turned and went back into the hallway.

It struck Allie that, if it was true that her father hadn't been drinking, then he had likely been the victim of a scam.

"I need to sit down." She started to walk over to the kitchen table, planning to pull out one of the chairs. She wished she could remember how her mother had handled things like this.

Allie scarcely noticed the steady arm Clay put around her. Then he lowered her into the chair like she was made of fine bone china. Once she was settled, he bent his head until his mouth was close to her ear.

"It'll be okay," he murmured.

"Those horses are never coming," she said, letting her troubles spill out to Clay like she'd done so often. "My father gave someone money, and he'll never see anything from it."

"That's my guess, too," Clay said.

Then in the distance Allie heard the sound of a heavily weighted truck coming.

She glanced up at Clay. He nodded to show he'd heard it, too.

"If that is them and they're here, that five hundred is probably only a down payment,"

Allie said. "I'll… We'll be paying for those horses for the rest of our lives."

She was still looking at Clay. Suddenly the years fell away and his face seemed the same as it had before. His eyes were the same warm blue. His eyebrow furrowed a little in concern. He looked like nothing was more important at that moment than what she was telling him.

"That's ranching for you," he said.

"We're flat broke," she told him and then stopped to listen as the truck slowed down at what must have been the cattle guard where their driveway came off the county road. "I don't even want to look."

"I'll see about it," Clay said as he straightened up.

Allie wondered if there was any possibility that the truck would go by on the gravel road. It was the long way around to the Redfern ranch, but maybe whoever was driving was lost and was just slowing down to ask directions.

She watched Clay. He hadn't moved from where he stood.

"We haven't even had breakfast yet," Allie said.

Clay grunted. "If it is those animals, we'll need to get them settled first."

"You're a good man," Allie said as she

sat there. "I have a little money saved. But not enough to pay standard wages to a ranch hand."

Clay smiled. "I don't think you're supposed to pay me. Free labor for a year. That's the deal."

Allie frowned. "We will make some arrangements. You can't work for free. I won't let you."

"It's fine," Clay murmured and then added hesitantly, "I think food is included, though. And I'll starve on toast."

She grinned. She saw the twinkle in his eyes. "Sorry about this morning. And you will get a full breakfast just as soon as we deal with that truck."

He smiled back at her, and her day tilted until everything felt balanced in her world again. She wished with a fierce stab of longing that Clay and her brother had stayed in the bunkhouse playing checkers that night.

"My dad's not really an alcoholic," she whispered at last. She hoped this was still true. "I wouldn't want you to think that."

"It's not your fault if he is," Clay said and buttoned his coat.

She shook off her nostalgia. "That's kind of you to say."

The truck sounds grew louder.

Maybe it wasn't all her fault, but Allie knew she'd fallen down on her duty. She had liked the warmth of Clay's breath on her neck, but there was nothing about this that was going to turn out well. She couldn't recall a thing her mother had done when her father's craziness had already happened except for doing all she could to hide everything from the neighbors.

She wondered how they could cope with a bankruptcy. They had fought it off for so long, but she was tired. She really would need to paint the house. She'd always thought white with green trim made a house look prosperous. That might keep the pity from the neighbors down some. Or at least give them some doubt that the gossip was true.

Allie heard a vehicle door slamming outside. Whoever was out there was coming inside. And she wasn't ready.

She looked up and saw compassion in Clay's eyes. She might not want him to know her father's weakness, but it felt good to have someone stand beside her in the troubles of this household.

Allie heard footsteps outside. She needed to remember that her goal these days was to see Mark recovered. Their family had been given a second chance. She wouldn't see alcohol or bankruptcy or problems from the past take it away from them.

Then her father cleared his throat. She looked over and saw him standing in the shadows of the hallway. His expression was so guilty that she wondered if there might be a bottle of liquor next to him in the coat closet.

"I should have asked you about the horses before I bought them," her father said.

Allie nodded. "We'll get by."

She forced herself to breathe calmly. She was only vaguely aware of the squeeze Clay gave to her shoulder before he moved toward the door. His brow was furrowed. His shoulders were hunched over in that sheepskin coat as though he was still cold even though it was warm in the kitchen.

A loud knock sounded at the kitchen door. Allie was relieved she didn't need to open the house and let anyone inside. Whoever was outside was going to give her trouble.

Chapter Four

Clay squinted as he opened the door. A sturdy middle-aged man, with a Stetson pushed down on his head and a red plaid shirt showing through the opening in his coat, waited on the steps with a clipboard in his gloved hands. Deep footprints showed where he had just walked through the snow. After studying the indentations, Clay guessed the snowfall was close to six inches deep. The man's black jacket had a logo and Farm Transportation embroidered on the front pocket, along with the name Stan Wilcox.

"This the Nelson place?" the man asked. His breath swirled up in a thin white puff. Even though the storm had stopped, temperatures had not risen yet.

"Yes," Clay admitted.

The man frowned and looked at his paper. "Mr. Floyd Nelson."

Clay realized with a start that he had never known Mr. Nelson's given name. He didn't remember anyone ever using it. "I'll get him for you. Stan, is it?"

The man nodded.

"I'm Clay West." He hesitated. "New ranch hand here."

"Good to meet you," Stan said.

Clay turned around then and saw that Allie and her father were walking toward the door. Clay opened the screen door for Stan. "Might as well come inside for a bit."

The other man entered and stood on the rug beside the open door. "We'll need to start unloading. I just wanted to check that we were at the right place and to find out where you want the shipment let down."

"Is it the horses?" Mr. Nelson asked as he walked closer.

"Yes, sir," Stan said. "This is them."

"I've been waiting." Mr. Nelson's face was as excited as a kid's on Christmas morning.

Clay smiled. The older man might be making a mistake, but he was at least enjoying it. Clay had to admit he wouldn't mind putting his hands on a horse again, either.

"I'll need you to sign." Stan held his clipboard out to Mr. Nelson.

Clay turned then and saw Allie walking over to the trucker and squaring her shoulders. He wondered for a moment about what she was doing.

"I'm afraid there is a change of plans," Allie said. Her voice was steady. "We need to send the horses back for a refund. I need to talk with my father some more, but we can't sign."

The man started to laugh.

"Someone will pay you for your delivery, of course," she added with a stiff smile. "Including the return trip. We honor our commitments as best we can."

Clay was proud of Allie. She'd obviously worked hard over the years to learn to speak her mind with confidence. He remembered how she'd hated to disappoint anyone and wouldn't confront them to say what she thought needed to be done.

Stan's laugh finally slowed to a rumble, and his eyes were kind. "That's not the problem, ma'am. These animals, though—there ain't no back to send them to. The man paid us in cash for the delivery, but then he got on a plane for Hawaii. Some messy divorce he's in. Didn't care how much money he lost. His ranch sold the day we left. He sent a few more animals over here with us. They were strays no one else wanted. If you don't want them, either, we'll have to shoot them."

"Goodness." Allie gasped. Clay saw the shock in her eyes. "We can't do that."

She turned to Clay, and he nodded in agreement. He knew how Allie was. She had taken injured birds and doctored them until they could fly again. She couldn't stand to see any animal hurt. She would never turn away an animal that needed saving. But Clay knew full well the problems that might be coming. He hoped none of the animals in the truck were ill.

"What do you need from us?" Clay asked Stan.

"For starters, just tell us where we should unload." Stan turned and opened the screen door. "We can sign the papers later. I'll tell my driver where he needs to park. Could take some doing, so you might as well stay inside for a few minutes. No point in all of us freezing."

Clay had never taken his coat off, so he was prepared. "I'll come give you a hand." He turned to Mr. Nelson. "Is the barn the best place to put them for now?"

The older man nodded. "The only place out of this cold. The weather report says the storm will continue off and on."

The kitchen door was opened again, and Clay stepped outside. He saw a long silver horse trailer and matching pickup sitting in the middle of the drive. A layer of snow had collected on top of the whole outfit. The sides were covered with dry mud, too, so Clay figured the vehicles had come some distance. In any event, he guessed it was too late to prevent any sickness from spreading if one of the animals had been infected with anything. They had all been together in that trailer.

"You're from Montana?" Clay asked as he walked down the steps with the other man. The sound of their leather boots was muffled by the snow. Clay liked the crisp air in his lungs. If the other man hadn't been in a hurry, Clay would have taken time to look around the ranch from where he stood midway between the house and the barn.

Stan nodded. "We came from over west by Helena."

Clay was glad that the trailer hadn't crossed any state lines. That might be complicated if there was illness in any of the animals.

A tall trail of exhaust rose from behind the pickup. Clay couldn't see much through the open slats along the sides of the metal trailer, but he saw dark shapes that were tall enough to be four horses.

"I'm assuming you have a ramp with you?" Clay asked Stan as they walked toward the vehicles. Clay wouldn't want to have to coax horses down a homemade ramp that was nothing more than several pieces of plywood laid one on top of the other. The ranch used to have something that worked pretty well, but he had no idea if it was still in the barn.

"We've got one built into the trailer," the other man said. "A couple of the horses are shy about using it, but we help them along."

Just then Clay heard a lot of flapping and squawking and the loud crowing of a rooster.

"Guess it's getting lighter inside the trailer," Stan said with a grin.

Clay noted that the sky was heavy gray still, but enough rays were getting through so that people—and apparently birds—could see.

"Big Red is waking up the crew," the other man added.

Clay heard the rooster again.

"You can't have chickens in there!" Clay muttered in protest. "I can't tell the guys I came here to babysit some old hens."

He'd forgotten about his few friends inside the prison, but suddenly he remembered his promise to send them postcards. They'd get a big laugh out of this. No one should get out on parole to tend poultry. He grinned some more at the thought of what they'd say when they heard.

What a day this was, Clay thought as he looked around. There were no telltale drips of snow melting off any roofs, but he supposed that would happen in a few hours if the temperature rose high enough. He heard the sounds of the front door opening, but when he looked, no one was stepping out to the porch yet.

"I suppose those birds are the animals you were going to shoot?" Clay asked. They were almost at the trailer.

Stan shrugged. "I was exaggerating a little about the shooting. I figure we can always give the chickens away. The woman at the café where we stopped to ask directions said she'd take them if nobody wanted them here. It's the goat that wouldn't find a home. He's an ornery old fellow. Name of Billy Boy. Thinks he's a dog. I can't believe how he tries to herd the horses. Him, we might have to shoot."

Clay groaned. "I think we can handle a goat."

Stan looked over at him. "Trust me, you don't want to cross him. He butts people when he feels it's necessary to protect his charges. I don't turn my back on him."

Clay heard steps on the porch and turned to

see Allie coming toward them. She'd walked several yards when Mr. Nelson came out of the door, holding Jeremy by the hand.

It would be a family welcome.

"The boss lady won't let anything be shot," Clay said, keeping his voice low so she wouldn't hear. "Don't even talk about it around her. Or around the boy."

"She'll want to keep the miniature pig, too, then?" Stan asked thoughtfully. He arched his eyebrow as he looked over at Clay. "It's a little black Juliana pig of the teacup variety. About eighty pounds. The missus in the divorce at that ranch had the pig for a pet. I hear they're worth a fair bit of money, but the husband got him in the settlement. Cute little thing. They call her Julie."

"Please tell me you have regular horses in there," Clay said. His confidence in this exchange was shaken. "Nothing miniature or with a pet name. This is a ranch for working horses."

Stan grinned. "Wish we did have a Shetland pony or something. My grandson would like that. But, no. The horses are full-size."

Clay nodded, but he knew better than to trust the man.

Stan called out to his partner behind the

wheel in the pickup. "We're going to put them in the barn over there."

Then he pointed out the structure as though there was more than one barn in view. The red slats on the sides of the barn were rough with age, but Clay knew it would do well enough.

The partner dutifully started the engine and began backing up.

Clay figured he had done all he could to keep the proceedings sane. He was beginning to think that Mr. Nelson had been right, though. The older man couldn't manage this menagerie. And he sure couldn't afford to pay anyone to do it. As far as Clay could see, most of these animals wouldn't bring any profit to the ranch. No, Clay was the only one to tend them.

Allie stood in the drive for a minute, her arms crossed to keep warm inside her corduroy jacket, as she watched the pickup maneuver the horse trailer closer to the barn. The old structure was in fair shape, she thought, but the corrals would need to be fixed. Patches of snow covered most of the ground, but coarse gray dirt poked up here and there. They would need feed for the animals. Her father had sold the last of his horses three years ago, and the ranch hands had been let go at the same time.

She mentally reviewed what might still be around and figured there were a few bags of old oats in the hayloft sitting on top of the plywood left after building the bunkhouse. The oats had probably gone moldy by now, but she'd check. She hadn't even gone out to the barn in over a year. With it empty, there seemed no reason.

They couldn't afford to feed a bunch of livestock for long. She'd already warned her father. They would have to sell the horses. As to the other animals that Stan had mentioned, she wouldn't send them to their deaths. But she couldn't afford charity. She'd work on finding other places for them.

Allie felt a twinge of guilt and then squared her shoulders. It was time she recognized that she didn't owe the whole world a living. She had enough to worry about with her father and Mark. And, Jeremy, of course, although he was nothing but a joy to her.

She looked over at where Clay was standing with Stan. A small frown crossed Clay's forehead. Dark stubble showed on his face. He probably hadn't shaved since he left prison. He looked tired. And it was only the beginning, she thought. Her father was right; they needed Clay for a while. What with the horses and Mark, they would be in a fix right now without him. Maybe after Easter, though, she could contact the parole board and find him another wrangler job near here. The Redfern ranch always seemed to need more workers. It would all work out.

Allie reached Clay about the same time that the pickup maneuvered the trailer into position.

"We'll need to close the side gate on the corral," she said, and Clay walked with her to do that. Then they opened the big barn door. The barn was like a large, dark cavern inside. A row of small windows was cut into each side of the barn, but the panes were dirty, and not much light filtered in, even on a sunny day.

"Smells musty," she said as she looked around. It was worse than she thought it might be. She should have at least aired it out when she came home to visit.

She heard the two men in the pickup setting up a ramp from the back of the horse trailer, and so she and Clay headed back to the front.

The rooster crowed again. This time Allie thought he sounded indignant.

"We haven't had a rooster around here for years," she said. They hadn't had hens, either. The ranch hands generally didn't like to tend to poultry, and they said the birds made the other animals nervous.

"He makes a good alarm clock," Clay said, glancing at her with humor in his eyes. "I thought you might not be too keen on him, though."

She smiled. "It'll give my dad a reason to get up and do the chores. I'll be in Jackson Hole, so I won't hear the rooster anyway."

Allie saw a flash of dark blue material in the corner of her eye and then heard her father grunt.

"I heard that," he said.

Then he came up beside them. "I don't need anyone to tell me when to do my chores. I've been working this farm for over sixty years."

Her father looked down at Jeremy, who stood beside him. "And this young fellow here is going to learn how to tend the animals, too."

Jeremy beamed as he leaned back and nodded.

"'ooster," the boy said with satisfaction as snowflakes landed on his face. "I like 'oosters."

Allie noticed Clay smile down at her nephew.

"They call him Big Red," one of the men said as the other one opened the back door of the trailer. "Not sure what breed he is, but he's a pretty fellow. The boy will like him. All those copper feathers."

By then the two men were unloading a crate

with what looked like a dozen white hens inside, although Allie had to admit it was hard to count with all the flying feathers and squawking. The men set that crate on the ground and pulled out a separate crate with the red rooster standing tall in it. One of the men turned and latched the trailer door behind them, and then the two of them started carrying the rooster's crate toward the barn.

"He goes first?" Allie asked.

"It is for the best," one of the men looked back and said with a chuckle.

Allie thought the golden red bird rode like an Oriental emperor, as though being carried along by two grown men was no more than what he was due.

"There's a chicken coop in the back of the barn," she called out. "You'll see the door on the right inside the barn. It goes to the coop. It's closed but not locked."

When the men disappeared into the barn, Allie turned to see that her father, Clay and Jeremy had all turned to stare at the open slats at the top of the trailer.

"Looks like Appaloosa horses in there," her father finally said.

"You didn't even know what kind of horses they were?" Allie asked in surprise.

"A man doesn't look a gift horse in the

mouth," her father said. "I knew they were good breeding stock and that the stallion has next-to-pure bloodlines. Like I said, it's mostly a favor to get them at all for the kind of money I paid. That's why the bank gave me a loan on them. They figured I couldn't go wrong."

Allie kept her mouth shut. She'd let her father enjoy his bargain horses. If they had to sell them, and she didn't see how they wouldn't need to, she would tackle that problem after Easter. If her father wanted to continue the Nelson family tradition of supplying the horses to pull the wagon that carried the Easter cross on Sunday morning, then they would keep the horses long enough to do that. She would have a week after that to find a buyer for the horses before she needed to head back to work.

Clay walked over to stand beside her. It took her a minute to realize the storm had started up again and that Clay was standing where he was because it broke the force of the wind hitting her. A flurry of snowflakes had already been falling. She could see it on his coat.

"You don't even have a scarf yourself," she protested. "I should stand in front of you."

"Not tall enough," he replied easily.

He stood there looking like he was having the time of his life; but his ears were turning red. He had left his hat inside, too.

She shook her head. "We'll go in once the horses are unloaded and fed. I think there are a few bales of hay left in the loft. And some oats. I'm not sure how tasty any of it will be after all this time."

They heard a commotion inside the trailer again. It sounded like something was thumping against the inside wall.

The two men came out of the barn and ran back to the ramp area.

"Sorry about that," one of them said, breathless. "Billy Boy doesn't like to be left behind."

The men moved with an urgency that made Allie curious. She turned to Clay. "I hope they're not talking about any of those horses. We can't have a wild horse around. Not with Jeremy here."

"I don't think it's a horse," Clay said with a small smile on his face as he watched the ramp.

Allie turned her head and heard the bleating of an animal.

"That's a—" She leaned forward until she saw the thing's head coming out of the back of the trailer. "A goat?"

She looked up at Clay, and he grinned.

"Yup, it's a goat," he said. "Apparently he has appointed himself bodyguard for the horses."

"Horses don't need that kind of help," Allie said as she watched the dark brown goat with a white star on his forehead pick his way down the ramp. His hooves were each outlined with black. He let his displeasure known with every shake of his head as he made the trip. "Those horns look sharp."

"That they do," Clay said. "We've been advised to keep on his good side."

Allie noticed that the goat's coat was shining and the animal looked well fed. At least her father hadn't bought animals that had been abused. When the goat reached the bottom of the ramp, he turned and looked back into the trailer.

"Don't they need to keep him on some kind of a tether?" Allie's father asked.

"I don't think so," Clay said. "Looks to me like he's waiting."

The cold had settled in around Allie, but she was too absorbed in the animal show to feel it much. She decided Billy Boy looked like he'd been in the military and with a rank of some command. She saw why he felt so important when the first horse put its head out the back of the trailer.

A gorgeous Appaloosa stallion took one step down the ramp and then stopped, as if trying to get a sense of where he was. The horse's shiny black coat covered the first half of him, and his hind half was white with a spattering of black spots the size of a quarter. His head was lifted proudly in the wind, and his mane blew gently.

Just when Allie began to wonder why the horse didn't continue his descent, she saw the goat walk over and climb back up the ramp slightly until he touched the foreleg of the stallion. The horse lowered its nose to the other animal's back. As the goat made its way down the ramp, the horse followed.

"What in the world?" Allie said as she looked over at Clay.

He'd been watching the duo, too. "I think the horse is blind."

"And the goat is what—like a Seeing Eye dog?" Allie asked, astonished. "I've never heard of such a thing."

Allie noticed her father and Jeremy walking closer to see the horse.

Clay didn't answer her question, and she saw he was watching another Appaloosa horse walking down the ramp. This one, a very pregnant mare, took delicate steps. She seemed hesitant and swung her head often. Again, the horse's coat was sleek and looked well tended. She was spotted all over, a creamy white with brown splotches.

"She's lovely," Allie said with an appreciative sigh.

"Something is very wrong," Clay countered,
frowning toward the ramp where a second Appaloosa mare was starting the descent.

"They look like someone took care of them,"
Allie said, turning to Clay. By now, the third
mare was descending the ramp. "I know that
only one of the mares looks pregnant, but the
other two might be due later. Maybe it says
something in that paperwork Stan has."

The third mare stood at the bottom of the
ramp, though, her head lifted like she was
hunting for some scent or sign. She nickered
softly and waited as though expecting a response.

"She's looking for the rest of the herd," Clay
finally said. "There had to be more than the
four of them, and she was expecting the rest
to be here."

As soon as Clay said it, Allie knew it was
true. The mare looked distressed.

"She misses her family," Allie said softly.

He nodded. "Wanting to be with one's family is only natural—even if they're no longer
there."

The driver of the pickup herded the mares
into the barn. Not that he had much to do since

they seemed inclined to follow the stallion and the goat.

"I never knew," Allie said softly. "If you missed your own family. When you came to our place."

She hadn't been very sensitive to Clay back then. He listened to all of her complaints and problems, but she didn't remember him ever talking about any of his troubles.

Clay shrugged. "It didn't help anything to miss my parents. They'd been gone a long time before I came here. I had no brothers or sisters. Not everyone needs a family."

Stan walked back to where Allie and Clay stood. Her father and Jeremy were still over by the corral, leaning against the poles.

"That's about it," Stan said. "Except the pig. I'll get her out now."

Allie was glad she'd have another moment with Clay. She wanted to say something even though she couldn't think of what it was yet.

"Those horses are blind," Clay said, making the man stay. "Why?"

Stan shrugged. "They have moon blindness. Not that uncommon in Appaloosas. Actually, the mares are only blind in one eye. It's the stallion that doesn't see at all. The ranch where they came from had a herd of over a hundred Appaloosas. These are the ones the buyer wouldn't take."

"So they were left behind," Allie said, her heart sinking. "They're used to a herd."

Stan shrugged. "They'll adjust."

Allie had no idea how to treat homesickness in a horse. Not that it would be the biggest challenge they faced. "How sick are they in their eyes?"

"If you treat them with corticosteroid drops, they'll get some better," Stan said. "At least I expect they will. We have what's left of the medicine with us, and we'll leave it. The rancher had us bring over what feed he had, too. You'll do fine for a couple of weeks."

Allie nodded. They would never be able to sell these horses. No one would buy them. The horses themselves had no hope of becoming part of a bigger herd. "How much do those drops cost?"

She wondered if she could pick up another shift at work. Or maybe she could get work as a waitress at the coffee place in one of the big resorts and pick up some extra hours that way.

"I don't know how much," Stan said, and he turned to leave.

Clay was quiet for a bit after the other man left.

"I never did ask," Clay finally said. He'd

turned to look down at her, his eyes serious. "Speaking of me coming here, why did your family ask for a foster kid back then?"

Allie smiled, remembering. "I was the one. My mother had died and I wanted—" She stopped then. She should have thought this through before she started her answer.

"You wanted what?" Clay asked. He didn't look like he could be put off, and she knew he wouldn't like it if she lied.

"I wanted a little sister. Someone to be silly with and do things like make cookies."

"I was to be your *playmate*?" Clay asked incredulously.

Allie shrugged. "They wouldn't give us a young girl because we didn't have my mother. They wouldn't give us an older girl, either. They thought any girl needed a mother in the house."

"So you ended up with me?" Clay asked.

He'd turned away so she couldn't see his face.

She put her hand on his arm. "I was never sorry that it was you who came."

By this time, Stan had put the horses in the barn and walked back up the ramp. He was bringing down what looked like a little dog now.

"I mean that," Allie said because Clay was still looking off into the distance.

"You don't need to worry about me," Clay said before taking a step toward Stan and that thing he was carrying. "I like my life."

"In *prison*?" Now it was her time to be baffled.

"I won't be in prison much longer," Clay said, staring at whatever Stan was carrying.

Allie realized it wasn't a dog when she heard the squeal.

"If you need money, you can always sell the pig," Stan added as he lifted the animal up so they could see it.

"This is Julie," Stan said like he was introducing them to royalty. "They call her a teacup pig because she's small. Only eighty pounds and she's full grown."

The black pig wiggled in the man's arms until she saw Allie. Then the animal lifted its head and inspected her.

"She's a princess all right," Stan said. "The woman of the house where we came from kept Julie inside the laundry room at night. Thought she was a guard dog. She's not, but her personality grows on you."

Allie just stared. "That's all of the animals, isn't it?"

Stan nodded and started to walk back to the barn.

Clay started to chuckle then, and she looked up at him. His laughter grew deeper, and his eyes danced with humor.

"You never know what you're going to get around here, do you?" he asked, his voice light and teasing. "One day a pig, another day a teenage boy."

"You were never a surprise like this," Allie interrupted, her voice firm. Then she saw his face and knew he was teasing.

"Oh," she said. "You."

"That goat looks dangerous and the pig way too intelligent for a barnyard animal," Clay continued.

Allie leaned over and whispered. "Shh—I don't think either of them see themselves as barnyard animals."

"Probably not," Clay agreed. "But they could mount a rebellion if they wanted. Mutiny in the cowshed. I can see it now."

Allie looked up and saw that her father was over by the corral signing the papers Stan had. When he finished, Stan sorted through them and peeled off a handful that he gave back to her father. Meanwhile, the other man had been pulling hay bales and sacks of grain out of the back of the trailer. He left everything just outside the barn door.

Stan started back toward Allie and Clay.

"We better get going," he said as his partner put the ramp up. "We want to get back on the interstate before the weather turns bad again."

Allie nodded. The wind had shifted again, and she didn't want to delay the men. "Thanks for the feed."

Stan reached out and shook hands with both Allie and Clay, then he ducked his head and turned around to jog back to the pickup.

By that time, her father and Jeremy had returned to where Allie stood.

"We better get everything inside the barn and dole some feed out to the animals," she said. Snowflakes were falling faster. "It's not going to get any warmer out here."

Allie heard the pickup and trailer drive out to the main gravel road as she led everyone into the barn. "It'll be quick work if we all do it. Then we can go inside for breakfast."

"With bacon?" her father asked eagerly.

"Just this once," Allie said as she opened the barn door.

"Nothing like a good crisp piece of fried bacon," her father said with a satisfied sigh. "The Nelsons have always liked their bacon."

"We shouldn't let Julie hear anyone say

that," Clay leaned over and whispered in Allie's ear. "It'll make her nervous."

"What?" She looked up and then she giggled. "No one would dare turn her into breakfast meat. She doesn't need to worry."

Allie had forgotten how much she and Clay used to tease back and forth.

It was warmer inside the barn than outside, but they still worked fast. The wind had gotten stronger and rattled some of the windows as they led each of the horses to a stall.

"As I recall there are a few horse blankets here somewhere," Clay said as he was rummaging through the tack room off to the side.

"I think they're up in the loft," Allie said.

Clay walked out of the tack room and headed for the ladder leading to the loft. "I can find them, if the rest of you want to go back inside the house. It's getting colder every minute. It'll probably be zero degrees out there before long."

"Maybe you should take Jeremy inside." Allie turned to her father. He should be inside in warmer temperatures, but she knew he wouldn't go for his sake.

Her father hesitated and then nodded. "Don't be long."

He took Jeremy's hand and led the boy out of the barn.

By this time, Clay had reached the hayloft and had several old horse blankets in his arms.

"Look out below," he said and then dropped them to the main floor before scrambling down the ladder.

"Stan said the horses had their eye medicine already this morning," Clay said. "If we scatter one of those bales of hay and put these blankets on their backs, they should do fine until I can get back out here later today and get the barn more organized."

"Cleaner, you mean," Allie said with a grimace. "I had no idea we had let it go so badly."

Clay shrugged. "I don't mind some dirty work." Then he looked down at the sheepskin coat. "I don't want to get this messed up, though. I wonder where it came from."

"My dad will know," Allie said. "But, don't worry. We have lots of old jackets in the house."

"I need to get that pump running, too," Clay said suddenly.

"I forgot about that," Allie said as she started walking over to back of the barn where the valves were. "The water's turned off, so it will take some doing to get it back on." She stopped to examine the water trough and pump apparatus before she even got to the valves. Everything was frozen. At least the pipes had been empty, so they hadn't burst. "Maybe we're best to carry a few buckets of water out from the house until we can get the pump set up again."

"I'll come back," Clay said.

"We'll both come back," Allie answered.

Clay gazed at her sternly, and Allie felt like looking away, but she didn't.

"I'm the hired hand." Clay smiled as he studied her. "You don't need to outwork me to prove anything."

"I'm not going to leave you with everything to do," Allie insisted. For some reason, she felt shy around him. "Especially when you are not getting paid."

"I plan to eat a lot," he said.

"Still," she replied.

"You never could take help," Clay muttered.

"Me?" she protested, but he only laughed.

Within a few minutes, they were both leaving the barn.

"That wind's coming faster," Allie said as she ducked her head down.

The barn door had been hard to open, and it slammed closed behind them.

Clay reached over and put his arm around her, drawing her closer to his side. "I won't let you blow away."

Allie knew he wouldn't. She had never felt as safe with anyone in her life as she had with

Clay. But she couldn't afford to lean on him. He'd broken her heart once when he left, and she didn't want him to break it again. That didn't mean she could let him do all the work, though.

Chapter Five

Clay felt invigorated as they fought the wind all the way to the house. He could move mountains with Allie tucked under his arm. He supposed it was nothing more than having a purpose in life again. One of the worst things about endless days in prison was the sensation of drifting, like it didn't matter whether he turned this way or that way in life. Now a few horses, a goat and a pig depended on him.

When Clay unlatched the screen door, he turned the knob on the main door as well so that Allie could hurry inside. She'd had her face pressed against his coat for the walk to the house, and when she stepped away he saw a long red mark on her cheek as a result. Her auburn hair had been whipped around her face and her lips were tight against each other.

"Cold," she muttered as she stepped into the warmth of the kitchen.

Clay joined her inside and closed the door behind them. They both stood on the rug by the door, stomping their feet and waiting for the tingling to stop in their fingers.

"It turned fierce out there all of a sudden," Mr. Nelson remarked as he came into the kitchen from the hallway on the other side of the room. He was in his stocking feet. Clay could see where the rancher had taken his boots off when he came inside and set them by the coat rack. A smaller set of boots was placed next to the older man's.

"Jeremy is in the back bedroom with that cat," Mr. Nelson continued, shaking his head. "He's worried she might be lonesome. I gave him a bowl of warm milk for the thing and fixed up a litter box."

Clay grunted. "I'm sure that old cat feels like she's landed in paradise."

"It's good for a boy to have a pet," Allie said from where she stood taking off her jacket. She'd patted her hair down already, and the red was fading from her face.

"That it is," Clay agreed, taking her all in— her tangled hair, bright cheeks and eyelashes that still shone with melting snow. She was beautiful.

Allie didn't respond and Clay figured he couldn't just keep looking at her, so he glanced around. When he'd been inside the house earlier it had been darker and he hadn't seen the place well. Now he saw it all. The walls were faded and needed paint. He had always imagined that this room was what a home looked like. The clock on the wall said it was eight o'clock. He used to wonder what it would be like to live in this house rather than out in the bunkhouse. Now he knew there had been trouble enough in here, too.

Clay was the first one to hear the distant sound of an engine. Initially, he thought the wind was merely changing directions and had found a drain pipe or something to make a whistling sound.

"I hope it's not those two guys coming back," Clay said when the sound grew louder and Allie had stopped to listen, as well.

"The deal is done," Mr. Nelson said. "They can't come back and get those animals. They're ours now."

"I'm sure they don't want them," Allie said, looking at her father with a touch of impatience. "I don't know how we're going to feed them, either."

"You'll figure it out," Mr. Nelson said, and there was nothing but confidence in his voice.

The stress seemed to have left the older man's face. Clay wondered if leaving everything to Allie to worry about always took the burden from her father. She did seem to be the one who shouldered most of the troubles around here. Now that Clay thought about it, it had been that way when he lived here long ago, too. Mark used to say Allie was a worrywart, always fussing about something. Clay suspected now that the story had been different. No one else had worried enough. She'd been taking care of them all.

A knock sounded at the door and a man shouted, "Anybody home?"

Clay knew he'd have to open the door regardless of who it was, but he wished the door had a window in it so he could see who it was before that. He didn't want to make the man wait, though, no matter what his business was. The temperature was too cold for that. Since the visitor wouldn't be for him, Clay stepped back as he opened the door until he was in the same half shadows that had hidden Allie earlier.

"Is he here?" the man demanded before he even stepped inside. The screen was still closed, but the man was peering through the mesh. Clay thought the voice sounded familiar, but he couldn't place it. The man continued, "Someone was sneaking through town with their lights on low an hour ago or so, and I figured it had to be him."

With that, Clay knew there was little hope the man was talking about anyone else but him.

"I wasn't sneaking," Clay said at the same time as Mr. Nelson spoke.

"Of course Clay is here," the older man announced as he walked toward the open door. "We're just getting him settled."

"Besides, it's a public road," Clay offered up in his defense. "And my headlights were on high."

The man grunted, and Clay left the shadows in hopes that he could take a better look at the visitor. "Randy Collins? Is that you?"

The tall, thin man swiveled. He was still on the other side of the mesh, so his lean face wasn't as clear as Clay would have liked. Some things had not changed, though. A worn black hat sat pressed low on the man's head and the collar of his red wool jacket sat up tight around his skinny neck. The sleeves on his jacket were too short, and his hands were shoved into his pockets. Randy considered it a sign of weakness to wear gloves unless it was twenty degrees below zero outside.

"It's me all right," Randy said with satisfaction in his voice.

Clay smiled. This man had been one of the ranch hands who lived in the bunkhouse with him. Clay didn't know why he was pleased to see Randy again. The two of them had never been particular friends, even if they certainly had gotten along easier years ago than it appeared they were now. Clay wondered if maybe it was the simple fact that they had shared a fire on many winter nights that made him want to avoid any quarrel with the man. There was not enough space in a bunkhouse for bickering.

"You're letting in the cold," Clay noted, keeping his tone mild as Randy just stood there. Clay might not want to upset the other man, but he didn't want to add to the difficulties he could see Allie already tallying in her mind.

Mr. Nelson stepped closer and spoke to Randy. "I expect you came out to welcome Clay here."

Randy snorted and finally opened the screen door. His breath still blew white in the freezing air.

"I'd rather welcome a blizzard," Randy muttered. "Or maybe even one of those freak tornadoes where everything goes flying."

"You got a problem with me?" Clay asked as the ranch hand walked into the middle of the doorway and stopped.

"You said it," Randy exclaimed and turned to point at Clay.

The man's finger was so pale it looked half-frozen. The door stayed open as Randy just stood there glaring.

Mr. Nelson grimaced and then waved the man inside. "Mad or not, you might as well get in here."

"I've done nothing for you to be getting on my case about," Clay said once the door was shut. Randy just stood there as the snowflakes on his hat and coat started to melt. At least he'd put his hands back in his pockets.

"You've caused me nothing but grief," Randy said, a hard note in his voice. "My life has fallen apart, and it's your fault."

"That's nonsense," Mr. Nelson reprimanded the other man sharply. "Clay hasn't even been here."

"I can speak for myself." Clay started turning toward Randy. He didn't get all the way there, though, when Allie walked past him, headed to the thermostat on the kitchen wall. Her face had more color than it had earlier. Just seeing her calmed him.

"I expect you have your challenges," Clay

said as he finished the turn and faced Randy. Clay had learned some conflict resolution tools in prison and he thought he should use them now. He tried to visualize himself in Randy's place, which was not easy to do when his gaze wanted to settle on Allie instead.

"I sure do," the other man agreed, not seeming to realize Clay had other things to occupy his mind.

Clay forced himself to concentrate.

None of the ranch hands had been comfortable coming to the big house, Clay thought as Randy took his hands out of his pockets and rubbed them together. That much hadn't seemed to change. Clay thought it looked like Randy had the same pair of boots that he'd had when they were working together. They were certainly creased and scuffed enough to be the same ones. His jeans were frayed, too. Life hadn't been prosperous for him lately.

Still, even if money was scarce, Clay wondered what could be that terrible about living as a free man in a place like Dry Creek. Randy might not be staying in the bunkhouse, but, if he was the one who had turned on that light Clay had saw in town earlier, he was set up in some house when Clay drove by tonight. The man had shelter and, likely, heat. Plus, there was lots of fresh air around. Good water. Enough quiet to think. Randy should try prison for a week, Clay thought to himself. That would teach him to be grateful for what he had.

Clay caught himself before he said anything. He supposed there were some problems in life for people who were not incarcerated, too. One of the key points in conflict resolution was to be open to the other person's experience.

"No need to get all upset," Allie said to the ranch hand as she walked toward the kitchen sink. She'd apparently warmed up. "Clay's going to be working with us for a while. That's why he drove out here."

"I can't see why you'd hire someone like him," Randy said, jutting his chin out in defiance.

Clay was going to say something, but Allie spoke to Randy. "You're welcome to stay for breakfast." Then she reached for the coffeepot and started the water running.

Randy looked surprised. "Thanks."

The men all listened to the water running for a moment.

"Anyway, I'm sorry if I disturbed you earlier," Clay finally managed to say. "We all need our sleep."

The other man shrugged. "I had to get up and check on things at the church anyway.

There are some kids that have been messing with the daffodil tarps. So far they haven't done anything but look. I saw tire tracks behind the building. I think it's mainly that foster kid over at the Redfern ranch. He'll do worse than look if we give him time."

"That's not fair," Clay protested, trying to keep his voice mild. He didn't want people here to be afraid of him. The fact that he had defended himself against tougher men than Randy didn't mean he should let that be known. "Just because a kid doesn't have a family doesn't mean he's up to anything wrong."

Randy grinned. "What else can you say? You guys all stick together."

"Being a foster kid isn't like being in a gang," Clay said flatly. His fingers had formed a fist, and he slowly relaxed them. Even when he was here he could have handled most of the men working on the ranch.

Randy snorted. "Oh yeah? The kid moves here from Missoula and suddenly trouble starts to happen around here. I don't know what you call it, but he's a bad influence on others."

"Does he wrestle?" Clay asked. "This boy."

Randy looked puzzled. "I don't know. Why?"

Clay shrugged. "A boy would need some muscle to make much trouble around here."

He remembered how people had their doubts when he moved here. "The teens here are big farm kids. No one tells them what to do—especially not some stranger. And they're not all perfect either. It could be any one of them doing stuff."

Randy eyed Clay. "I remember you said something like that to the judge at your trial. You led Mark down a path of crime, and when the whole thing went south, you blamed him. Always pointing to the other guy."

"I happened to be telling the truth," Clay said and took a deep breath.

He glanced over at Allie. She looked tired. Tendrils of her dark auburn hair fell from the twist she had in the back of her head. She had picked up the spatula again. He wondered if she was going to fry some eggs.

"You're just making excuses," Randy said, scoffing.

Clay felt his heart start to speed up. He knew how to keep his cool. But, it didn't mean that he didn't still get angry.

"Now, boys," Mr. Nelson said, sounding old and weary.

"Dad's not supposed to have any stress," Allie interjected from where she stood by the stove. "High blood pressure."

"Are you okay?" Clay asked the rancher.

Mr. Nelson nodded.

"He'll be just fine when you get yourself out of here," Randy said. "When are you planning to leave?"

"Not for some time." Clay didn't like how pale Allie's face was. "I have some things to do first."

"Like what?" Randy asked belligerently.

"Visiting someone," Clay replied.

Randy's eyes narrowed. "Who? There isn't anyone here who you need to see."

"My brother," Allie said then. "If you have to know, he's going to see Mark."

"Well," Randy started in the same tone and then stopped. He continued in a much quieter tone. "Don't seem much point to that, sorry to say."

"I don't agree," Clay said firmly.

Allie looked over at him in alarm. "Remember."

Clay nodded but didn't say anything else.

"The two of you are in cahoots, aren't you?" Randy asked, a quiet edge to his voice as he jerked his head in Allie's direction.

Clay wasn't sure what the other man was implying, but he kept his voice neutral. "Allie has a right to speak up around here. This is her home."

"And we're only the hired help," Randy shot back. "You best remember that."

Clay flinched. The other man wasn't saying anything Clay didn't know, but he didn't like to hear it.

"You might as well spit it out," Clay said then, knowing there was more poison to come from the man.

Randy nodded and lifted the finger he had pointed at Clay earlier. "You are the one to blame. Always have been. The boss here took you in when he didn't need to all those years ago. Not all of us in the bunkhouse thought it was a good idea. But he did it—out of the goodness of his heart. And what did you do? You brought this ranch to its knees. Clean wiped the Nelsons out. There's nothing left out there. And me? I lost my job because of you and haven't found another once since."

Clay had been told by the social worker who brought him to the ranch that everyone was on board with the decision, but Clay had wondered at the time if that were true. He wasn't going to apologize, though, so if that was what the other man was waiting for, they would be standing here for a long time.

"It wasn't just me—" Randy started in louder now that Clay was silent.

"Who wants bacon?" Allie called out and

interrupted the other man. Clay could have kissed her. She was the peacemaker. Everyone paused and assured her that they did want a few slices.

Mr. Nelson walked to the table and sat down in a chair. Then he looked at Randy and motioned him to the table, as well. "Is this about your cousin? Is that what has you stomping around?"

"For starters," Randy admitted as he joined the other man. He took his hat off and slapped it on the side of his leg to dislodge the few flakes of snow that hadn't melted yet. Then he set the Stetson on a side chair.

"Sam Collins is his cousin," Mr. Nelson announced to Clay and then pulled out a chair at the table for Clay. "You remember him?"

Clay nodded. He'd never forget the clerk at that gas station who had spoken out against him at his trial.

"He's never gotten over the shooting that happened that night," Randy said accusingly as he sat there. "Now he won't take a job in any service station. Too afraid of being robbed again. Can't seem to get any other kind of a job, either. Not even pizza delivery. He moved back to his parents' old house. Nobody had lived in it for years. Had to take the boards off the windows. All he's got for money is the rent I pay for staying with him in the house."

"I remember you talking about your cousin." Clay didn't move closer to the table like the other two men had. "Always sounded like you got along together fine."

"We did. I mean, we do," Randy said, moving his hat from the chair to his knee. Maybe because he was getting warmer, the red in his face had lessened. "But my cousin can't get by without what little I pay him in rent, and I don't want to spend my life living with him. I feel like we're still kids together. The time comes when a man's got to have a place to call his own. A home, you know. Some place where he could set up a family."

Randy's face flushed a deep red. "You know how it is. A woman would refuse to even date a man with no job and nothing but a room in his cousin's house."

"Ah," Clay said. Now he understood.

"Come to think of it, I don't suppose you would know about that," Randy said. "The dating I mean."

Clay shrugged. "There are guys in prison who have women who write to them and propose. We're better than a dating service."

Randy shook his head but gave a wry chuckle. "You're a regular a comedian, aren't you? Or are you saying I should go rob a bank to improve my chances with women?"

"I'm just saying you shouldn't give up," Clay said, and then he looked over at Allie. "Isn't that right?"

Allie smiled. "Leave me out of this one."

Clay imagined she was smiling straight at him. She always had appreciated his joking around. It suddenly struck him that he was as bad off as poor Randy here, wishing for what he didn't have.

"You won't think this is so funny when you lose your job and it happens to you," Randy said to Clay then, back to being glum.

"I didn't mean to make light of it," Clay said, sobering. "I know a man needs a job."

"He sure does," Randy said, giving Clay a defiant look before turning toward Mr. Nelson. His voice lost any belligerence it had and became subservient as he addressed the older man. "Just want you to know that if you need a ranch hand, you don't need to rely on Clay there. My job taking care of those daffodils for the church is just until Easter. They don't pay much. It's not even really a job. I think they just have me doing it so they can give me some money, and I'll take it. But it's something so I can take partial wages until you get the ranch going again. I can still pay some rent to Sam if I live in the bunkhouse. We'll work it out."

Clay supposed he shouldn't be surprised that one of the old ranch hands would be circling his new position like a hungry vulture waiting for its prey to stumble and die. Clay knew how to stop that, though. "I'm not getting any wages."

Randy seemed taken back at that announcement. "Are they holding your money back until harvest or something?"

Clay shook his head as he walked over to the table. He still didn't sit down. "It's called victim reparations. I don't get paid—ever."

Randy looked like he was taking a minute to digest that information.

"So, if you want the job," Clay said softly, "it's all yours."

Randy didn't answer.

Clay walked over to the stove and held out his hand to Allie. "Can I help?"

She looked up at him in surprise before giving him the platter of eggs and bacon to take over to the table. A dish towel had been put under the plate like a pot holder, and he welcomed the warmth in his hands as he carried the food.

"I'll bring the coffee," Allie said as she lifted up the plate of toast, as well.

Clay nodded.

"Thanks for helping," Allie murmured as they walked together.

Randy frowned over at Clay. "You wear an apron these days?"

Clay didn't say anything as he started walking to the table. "I sure do if I can find one. Nothing wrong with a man helping in the kitchen. Especially if he wants to eat."

Randy scowled even deeper.

Clay and Allie set their platters on the table and then each sat down.

Allie had to admit she'd been as surprised at Clay's actions as Randy had been. Cooking was still considered women's work in this ranching area. She didn't remember Clay ever offering to help with kitchen chores when he'd been here before. Maybe he had learned a thing or two in prison.

"Let's pray before we get to the eggs and bacon," her father said then as a fully dressed Jeremy raced to the table and found his chair. Allie noted he'd found the blue shirt he'd been looking for. She looked closer and could see the cat hair on it.

Allie saw her father reach out his hand to her and then Jeremy. The boy held out his hand to Randy.

"After Grandpa prays," Allie whispered to Jeremy, "you'll need to go wash your hands. One of the rules of having a pet is to wash your hands before you eat anything."

Jeremy nodded.

"We hold hands as we pray," Allie then turned to her side and murmured to Clay. When he'd been here before, the ranch hands had their meals out in the bunkhouse. Her father had said it was too much work for Allie at her age to cook for eight working men in addition to the family. They had put in a full kitchen out there, and one of the older men had fixed the meals.

She offered Clay her hand.

For a minute, Allie thought he wasn't going to take it.

"I hope it doesn't offend you if we pray," she whispered, feeling awkward with her hand still stretched out. She sometimes neglected going to church when she was working in Jackson Hole, but she never did in Dry Creek. She knew prayer worked; her mother had taught her that. She was grateful she could pray with her family.

"I wouldn't say it offends me." Clay finally reached out, as well. "I'm used to doing for myself so I sure don't count on prayers to do much good, but I don't mind folks asking for help."

Before she knew it, he had her hand securely tucked inside one of his. She could feel the cold from him still even though he'd been inside for a while now.

"I think one hand is enough, though," Clay said quietly with a smile at Randy. "No offense if I don't take yours."

"None taken," Randy said with some relief in his voice.

"We need to pray for the mama kitty," Jeremy said as he looked up at his grandfather with trust in his eyes. "So she knows I'm her friend and will feed her. I think she's still a little scared."

Allie smiled at her nephew. "You'll need to be patient with her. Is she drinking the milk Grandpa gave you for her?"

Jeremy nodded.

Her father's prayer was simple, and it calmed her. As she sat with her eyes closed and listened to him ask for God's blessing on those animals he'd just bought, she prayed for her own strength. She could not blame her father for wanting his ranch to be active again. It's just that she was paying those mortgage payments and she didn't know how she'd stretch things to include more.

"And we thank You for Your bounty to us." Her father's voice interrupted her thoughts.

"Amen." Allie joined him in saying the word.

The smell of bacon and fried eggs hung in the air until breakfast was finished.

"I appreciate the meal," Clay said as he pushed back his chair and rose. "I'd like to take a look around the barn and see what's what, though, before too much time passes."

"You'll want to look at the bunkhouse, too," Mr. Nelson said, looking up to meet Clay's eyes. "It'll make you want to sleep in the house tonight. You can take Mark's old room. Jeremy's using it now, but he can sleep on the couch. I didn't get anything out there straightened up."

"The bunkhouse is fine for me," Clay said as he walked over to the rack and lifted the sheepskin coat off it. "It looks like this storm isn't going away, so I'd like to get settled in out there anyway."

Allie watched as he stood there a moment. Then he turned toward her and her father.

"I never did hear who this sheepskin coat belongs to," Clay said.

Allie noticed he didn't ask outright, but he was clearly curious.

"Oh, I forgot," Mr. Nelson said. "I was supposed to tell you that the coat belonged to Mrs. Hargrove's first husband. He's been dead for a long time now, and she thought you might need a warm coat. Told me to have it sent over with the pickup. You know Mrs. Hargrove, don't you? Well, a few years ago she married my cousin, Charley Nelson, but she keeps her old name."

"She didn't want to confuse all the little kids in Dry Creek," Allie added. "She'll always be Mrs. Hargrove to them."

"She's a good woman all right," Clay agreed as he stood looking at the coat in his hands. "She wrote to me in prison, and I appreciate that. Which is all the more reason for me to borrow something else to wear while I clean out the barn. I'll save the coat to wear to church tomorrow."

"It'd look nice with a good tie," Allie teased.

Clay grinned back at her. "Ties are not real popular in prison. Neither are belts or shoelaces. I do have a good shirt, though."

Allie couldn't manage a smile in return. She suddenly didn't like the thought of Clay being in a prison. There was nothing amusing about that.

"We have some things in the spare closet," she said as she led Clay into the hallway.

Allie remembered that her mother had always complained that the hallway was too small and too dark. They'd done what they could by painting the walls a mint green that her mother claimed would remind everyone of spring. Several pencil drawings were framed and lined up between two doorways. She noticed Clay studying the artwork, but he didn't say anything.

"Some cousin drew them," she finally mumbled as she slid the closet doors open and reached inside. "My mother liked them."

"They're good," Clay said sincerely.

"Here are a couple of the extra work coats." Allie held up a red parka and a brown wool coat. Both were a little ragged. She held the parka higher. "Mark wore this one in high school. Said it was warm enough for skiing—not that he ever got a chance to go. My dad uses it some now."

Allie almost put the jacket back in the closet. It wasn't fair that her brother never even had a chance to ski down a mountain.

Clay reached for the jacket, though, and she let it go.

"Let's see if it fits," he said. "It looks like the bigger of the two, but—"

Clay started to shrug his shoulders into it. He didn't have it all the way on when Allie heard the sound of fabric tearing.

"Oops," she said as Clay froze in position.

"Here, let me see what's wrong," Allie said as she hung the brown coat back on a hook in the closet. The light in the hallway might be dim, but she could see a pucker in the back of the red parka, and she reached her hand out to feel along the seam of the coat.

"It's the lining, I think," Allie said as she lifted the back of the coat up as far as she could. That left a broad expanse of gray plaid flannel shirt covering Clay's back. Frayed threads from a tear in the red nylon lining of the coat stuck to the shirt. Allie laid one hand on Clay's back to steady herself while she picked the few threads off Clay's shirt. It was a mistake. The heat coming from him made her pull her hand away.

Suddenly, the hallway seemed even darker than it had been. It was all in her mind, she told herself. She was more than eight inches from Clay West's back, and she needed to collect her wits.

"I'll be able to mend that for you," Allie said, hoping her voice didn't give away her agitation. She supposed she was having a temporary flashback to her teenage years. She certainly felt like the love-struck sixteen-year-old girl who had a crush on Clay.

"You've grown," she said without thinking

as she smoothed the coat down over his back. Even with all of the padding in the coat, she could feel the strength of his muscles. She let her hands drop when she realized she was almost caressing him.

He turned around. She hoped he didn't see the pink in her face.

"You don't need to fix the coat on my account," Clay said, his voice low and uneven. "I just need it to clean the barn. The tear isn't very big."

Allie thought Clay sounded rattled. She hoped he hadn't wondered what she was doing leaving her palm against his back like that. She didn't know if she could explain it.

"You'll need a scarf, too," she said, leaving the closet door open. "On the hook to the right. There are a bunch of them."

She could see Clay nod.

Allie hurried back into the kitchen. Randy was standing beside the table.

"I'll be going," the ranch hand said when he saw her. "Thanks for breakfast."

"Come back later if you want to work a few hours today," Allie said impulsively. "We'll have work for a couple of days next week, too. We're going to need help getting the barn and corrals ready for all the animals. An extra pair of hands will help. Especially with Sunday coming up tomorrow. It won't be long, but we can pay an hourly wage."

"Great," Randy said, a smile splitting his face. "I'll go back to my cousin's and get some work clothes. I have a few other things to take care of for the church, but I'll be back by noon."

Randy had his hand on the outside door as Clay walked back into the kitchen from the hallway. He had a mud-colored wool scarf twisted around his neck.

Clay walked out of the door behind Randy and closed it. Allie could still see his shape through the screen door, and she watched him head toward the bunkhouse.

"I wonder if he realizes that he picked that pink scarf," her father said, a smile on his face. "At least the wool was pink before you dyed it. I believe you knitted that the winter when you were twelve."

Allie nodded and scrunched up her nose. "That was when I decided pink was for girls and I wanted to be more…" She shrugged.

"You wanted to be one of the guys." Her father supplied the rest of her words.

"It seemed to work back then," Allie said.

It was odd that Clay had chosen that scarf. She generally kept it as far back in the closet as she could. It was the ugliest scarf she'd ever seen.

"And now?" her father asked quietly.

Allie looked up in surprise. Her father never wanted to talk about feelings and things like that. She wondered suddenly if he had seen her standing in the hallway with her hand on Clay's back. She'd no sooner asked herself if that could have happened before she decided it was meaningless anyway. It wasn't like they had kissed or anything.

"I could wear pink now," Allie answered her father.

He nodded. "That's what I thought."

She didn't say anything else as she put on her own coat and scarf. "I best go help. Keep an eye on Jeremy."

"We'll come out in an hour or so," her father added.

"Randy might be back by then," Allie said as she headed for the door. "You and Jeremy might as well spend the morning inside. The boy doesn't need all this cold."

Her father nodded. She couldn't help but wonder if he was giving her some time alone with Clay.

Her father's color was beginning to look

normal again. The temperatures were too low for him out there, so she hoped he would be content to stay with Jeremy.

Chapter Six

The sky was still overcast when Clay walked out of the house and headed to the bunkhouse. He noticed a small drift building in front of the pickup as he walked by. Damp air chilled him as he breathed it in, but the cold helped settle him. He told himself he needed to call a halt to the feelings he was starting to have. The one thing Randy had gotten right this morning was that they were both workers on this ranch. Allie was the owner's daughter. He and Allie had always had a certain something between them, but that didn't mean she was interested in him as anything more than a ranch hand.

The snow was deep on the steps to the bunkhouse, and Clay used his boots to open up a wide pathway. When he tried to open the door, it would not budge. The knob turned, but the door was stuck.

"I'm guessing the latch is frozen. Ice," Clay muttered to himself. Nothing happened easily around here, and that was fine with him.

He put his shoulder to the door and pushed. It opened.

Light came into the bunkhouse through the side windows. He barely noticed the layer of dust on the plank floor of the long room. Everything was brown in the shadows. Seven metal cots lined the north wall, nails sticking out of the raw wood boards above each short headboard. An old shirt that used to be white and was now gray hung from one of the nails, and the other homemade hooks looked ready to hold more belongings. The cots were still neatly made with the top of the white sheets folded back over khaki blankets. There were no pillows.

Clay eyed the last bunk in the lineup. That one had been his. No nails had been hammered into the wood above that cot, which made him realize that his cot had been added later than the others. He had squeezed the other ranch hands when he moved in. None of them had said anything, though. He wondered now what other cues he'd missed back then.

Like with the other cots, the top blanket on his went to the floor on both sides, so he couldn't see under it. He did wonder briefly if his old suitcase was still there. No one had mentioned his belongings when they sent him off to jail. He had never heard what had happened to that suitcase. Someone had probably thrown it out by now. It had been with him for all twelve of his years in the foster care system, but it didn't look like much so he didn't think anyone would hesitate to toss it. It had been where he'd kept his drawings, though.

By now he could see through the window that Allie was walking over here, picking up her feet in the packed snow like she was walking through a layer of thick sand. That meant the snow must be melting a little. Clay would look under his old cot, but he didn't want to be going through those drawings when she was around. Too many of his drawings had been of her. The thought of her seeing them made him hope someone had thrown that suitcase away without bothering to open it. Not that there was anything improper in the drawings; they were just starry-eyed. As he remembered, he'd even drawn roses around the border of one of her portraits.

He shook his head just thinking about it. He supposed every man had a sentimental streak when he was young. That didn't mean he wanted anyone to know about it, though.

Clay moved deeper into the room. A rock

fireplace dominated the wall by the outside door. There were still ashes in the grate and a glass canning jar on the simple pine mantel. Three brown leather sofas were gathered in front of the fireplace. A scarred coffee table stood in the middle of them, and a pole lamp stood to the side.

Clay remembered some good times, sitting around that fireplace in the evenings with the other ranch hands. Sometimes the cook would make them all cocoa when a blizzard was howling outside.

He continued gazing around and saw the door to the left that opened up into what everyone had called the new kitchen when he'd been here. It had been added to the bunkhouse a few months before he got there. A new large bathroom had been added, as well. He walked over and looked into the kitchen. Black-and-white linoleum covered the floor. A long counter lined the wall across from the door, its length interrupted by the double sink in the middle. The dark green countertop was tile. The cabinets had been painted white. Two regular-sized refrigerators sat to the left of the door, and a double-oven gas stove was on the wall opposite.

Large square windows dominated the far white corner of the kitchen, and that's where the rectangular oak table sat, three chairs to each side and one on each end. In the winter, when the shades were rolled up, that was the warmest corner in the bunkhouse, including the sofas by the fireplace. A bookcase stood under the left window, not that there were many books. The ranch hands joked that the bookcase was nothing but a fancy display for the cook's philodendron plants. Clay and Mark used to sit in that corner, playing chess at the table and discussing the problems of the world.

Clay looked closer and remembered the Bible that stood in the bookcase. He and Mark had been doing something called the Easter Challenge that year. The church had invited everyone to read the Gospel of Luke.

Clay went over and slipped the Bible off the shelf. Mark had his own Bible in the main house; this one had been left behind by some ranch hand Clay never knew. The gum wrapper he'd used to keep his place in the Bible was still there. As he recalled, neither he nor Mark had gotten very far in the story before that night interrupted both their lives.

Clay set the Bible back where it had been, noting for the first time that the shelf had rust rings where metal planters had sat for years. Someone must have eventually thrown the planters away.

He heard the door open in the other room, and he turned slightly.

Before long, Allie stood in the doorway of the kitchen. She had a loose knit scarf around her neck, the red of the scarf making her cheeks look even pinker than they did from the cold. Allie always had liked color.

She looked around and shook her head. "I thought we at least had some pictures on the walls out here. It's pretty dreary. We'll fix it up for you."

Clay shrugged. "I've lived with worse. It's okay."

He knew he'd said the wrong thing when he saw Allie's face crumple a little.

"We're not going to let you live in a place that's as bad as prison," Allie said, her voice firm. "You can stay in the house." She paused and added softly, "In Mark's old room."

Clay looked at her. He'd seen less resolute faces on men headed to solitary confinement. "There's no need for that. You've no reason to feel guilty."

Her eyes flashed at that. "The least we can do is see that you have a nice room. I figure other parolees get paid for the time that they work for someone."

"I wouldn't know," Clay said shortly.

"You might have ended up with a regular

parole if it wasn't for my father," Allie said in a rush.

Clay was silent.

"It's the truth then?" Allie said as her shoulders slumped and she stared at the floor.

Clay hated seeing her look miserable. And it certainly wasn't justified. "I never qualified for parole."

Allie looked up at that.

"Before you can be considered for parole, you have to say you are sorry for what you did," Clay continued quietly. "I never did what they said I had so—"

Clay couldn't take his gaze off Allie. As he watched, her eyes grew round.

"You wouldn't admit it," she finally said. "Not even to get out of prison."

The silence between them stretched long.

Finally, Allie shifted her stance. More light was coming in the windows, and it sounded like the wind had died down outside. She had known Clay was proud and stubborn, but she almost couldn't believe what she was hearing.

"When would you have gotten out on parole?" she asked then. "If you had done what they asked?"

"Last year about this time," he said.

Allie nodded for lack of anything else to do.

"Please, do take Mark's bedroom if you'd like. It's much warmer in the house."

Clay shrugged. "I'm guessing Mark's room has been kept for him, just the way he left it."

Allie nodded. Her father had insisted on that, and she had half agreed with him so neither one of them had disturbed it much. They even left his comb on his dresser and the books he was reading on his nightstand. She had changed the linens before Jeremy came, but no one else had stayed in the room in the past four years.

"Jeremy can sleep on the airbed in my dad's room," Allie continued. "He spends half of the night there anyway. He likes to sleep with his grandpa."

She could see Clay considering her words.

"Thank you," he finally said. "But I'd do better out here. I'm sure there's firewood out by the back door, and we'll be able to turn the water on today. Randy might want to stay in the bunkhouse, too. It'll be like old times."

He was trying too hard to convince her, Allie thought, but she wouldn't argue. "I'll take the bedding in and let that go through the washing machine while we're working in the barn. You'll have your meals with us no matter what."

Clay looked relieved when she accepted his

decision. She supposed he might like the solitude of the bunkhouse after being in prison.

"I suppose we should see to the animals first," she finally said. "Once we have some hot water to work with, I'll run the mop over these floors, as well."

Clay nodded. "Let's go to the barn then."

Allie followed him as he walked out the door.

The number of things she was responsible for was growing, she told herself. She missed her mother. She had spent her childhood trying to control more than she could with her father and brother. She wasn't about to become involved with a man she could not trust.

Which reminded her of something.

"My father has a note for you," she said to Clay as they approached the barn. "He wanted me to be sure and take you back to the house before Randy got back. He thought the note might be private."

"Private?" Clay stopped and turned around. "For me?"

Allie nodded. "I didn't ask from whom."

Her father liked to be secretive, but she wished he had given her some clue. She could tell Clay looked worried. She wondered if there was any way the parole board had sent him a message telling him to come back. She knew she should want something like that to happen, but she didn't.

Clay was here, and he seemed to want to stay. At least, she thought so.

"We should get things set up in the barn first," Clay said. "Let's check on the pump. And we should turn the propane heater on here in the bunkhouse and in the tack room off the barn."

"I'd like to take another look at the Appaloosa horses, too," Allie said.

"I knew you couldn't resist those horses," Clay said, grinning. "They'll eat you out of house and home, but you're going to like having them here."

Allie didn't even bother to reply. She'd forgotten how well he'd known her when he lived on the ranch. It would be easy to step back into their old friendly ways. But that robbery had changed everything. She didn't know if she could ever trust him again.

Chapter Seven

Allie stepped into the barn before Clay. Sunshine streamed in through the windows and the air vents until there were rectangular blocks of light throughout the barn. The smell of sweet hay mingled with that of horse. None of the Appaloosas turned to look at Allie and Clay when they walked farther into the barn, but Allie noticed the goat, Billy Boy, stood next to the stallion and gave them a warning bleat.

"We're harmless," Allie said to the goat.

Billy Boy dipped his head, but didn't make another sound.

Allie let the silence surround her as she watched Clay walk toward the animals. When he came to one of the mares, he held his hand out.

"Easy now," he whispered as he ran his hand along the mare's spotted flank.

Allie could sense how much Clay liked being with the horse. Chocolate-brown splotches mixed with the light cream of the animal's coat.

Clay looked over the horses back to the water trough and turned to Allie. "Looks like the pump is working."

Allie nodded. She felt like she had come home in a way that she hadn't felt in years. The Nelson ranch had always had horses. Even though she didn't like the way her father had done things, she couldn't be sorry that these horses were here.

She walked over to a different mare from the one Clay had claimed. She made sure she was on the right side of the mare so the animal could see her out of the one eye that seemed to be working.

Allie ran her fingers across the sway in the back of the young mare. The horse backed away and nickered a little. Allie took her hands off the animal and waited until the mare came close again. Allie rested her hand on the mare's back this time without moving it. She could feel the nervous tension in the horse.

"Easy," she murmured as she started to stroke the horse again. A riot of gray spots covered the white coat of this one. She had always liked Appaloosas; they were like some impressionistic painting hanging in a museum. They used to be the horse favored by the Plains Native Americans, too, so they were in their share of famous artwork.

"Those spots on her look like smoke going up a chimney," Clay commented to Allie as he studied the horse she was working with. "Wonder what her name is."

"The only information in the paperwork about the horses are numbers," Allie answered. "The horses were stock, not pets. I doubt they have names."

"Even the goat has a name," Clay said. "I can't see calling the horses by numbers."

"They were part of a larger herd," Allie said. "No one names a hundred horses. But for these, it's going to change." Allie stroked the mare's neck. "Isn't that right, Zee Zee?"

Clay looked over at Allie in surprise. "I figured you'd go with something like Spot. You know, an animal's name. *Zee Zee* sounds like a rock star."

Allie pointed to the mare's neck. "Doesn't that cluster of spots form a *Z*?"

Clay nodded. "Close enough."

"Besides, she's a classy lady," Allie added as the mare finally turned to her and nuzzled her hand. "One who expects a little sugar now and then."

Clay was silent as Allie kept petting the mare's neck. Finally, she looked over at him. He was staring at her like he was puzzling over something.

"What?" she said.

"I always wondered what a classy lady would want," Clay said with a wry twist to his mouth. He had walked closer and no longer stood by the mare he'd singled out earlier.

Allie felt her mouth go dry. She worked so many hours in Jackson Hole that she didn't date. She was, however, used to men flirting with her. That seemed a perennial problem for any woman who worked in the ski resorts. She'd handle this the same way she would if she were on the job.

"What do ladies want?" Allie stopped stroking the horse. More sunshine was coming into the barn, but it was still dim enough for the barn to feel intimate. She waited an extra moment to be sure she had his attention. "Most of the ones I know want someone to clean up around the house."

Clay grinned. "I thought it was diamonds."

"That, too," Allie said, flashing him a cocky look. She was relieved he had been teasing.

"Well, that leaves me out," Clay said then as he started walking to the barn's door. The wood floor echoed with each step of his boots.

Allie fell into step with him as he passed. She wore tennis shoes and she made no sound.

She told herself she had handled that well. She supposed it was only natural that she and Clay would flirt with each other a little until they found their rhythm again. They had both grown up since they had been friends before. Their lives had changed. Yet some of their teasing still seemed to be in place.

As Clay reached for the barn door handle, Allie decided she might as well ask the question she wanted answered.

"But how about you?" she said. "What is it that you want? I mean, with your girlfriend."

He hadn't mentioned any woman, but Mark always said Clay had women coming on to him all the time. She'd spent her sixteenth year jealous of phantom girls who she never knew even existed. It wasn't wrong, she told herself, to want to know if her old friend had a connection with someone.

Clay stopped and considered a moment. Then he turned and looked directly at her. The dim light in the barn darkened the blue in his eyes. His lips quirked slightly, and he reached out to gently touch her cheek. She parted her lips as he trailed his finger down her cheek until it rested near her lips. He leaned downward in slow motion, and she arched up on her tiptoes.

He kissed her, and Allie felt the warmth of it curl inside her. It was the gentlest kiss she'd ever had, scarcely more than a brush of his lips, but she didn't want it to end.

Clay rested his forehead against hers for a few moments before eventually pulling away.

"All I want is for someone to trust me," he whispered. "To believe me and know what I say is true."

"Oh." Allie knew then that this had also been the saddest kiss she'd ever had.

"I'm not sure if I've met her yet or not," he whispered.

"I can't choose you over Mark." She felt a moment's anger that he would ask that of her, and then she remembered she had been the one to bring up the question.

"I'm sorry," she added.

"So am I," he answered.

He pulled away then, and they stood there looking at each other.

She knew without asking that he would not compromise on this point. They were on opposite sides here.

Clay finally moved to open the door, and they walked out of the barn. The midmorning sun had warmed everything outside. The snow was melting, and that made it even harder to put one foot in front of the other.

Sometimes, Allie told herself, a woman had to stick with her family even if her heart wished she could believe something improbable. That was part of being a grown-up. Things did not always go the way one wanted. That night could not have happened the way Clay remembered. But he'd been tried and convicted of armed robbery. The court might have some doubt that Clay was the one who planned the holdup, but for the past four years, Allie had refused to believe her brother had been the one to do so. Clay had to be the one most at fault. If only Clay would admit it, she could forgive him.

Chapter Eight

The gray clouds were leaving and the sky was turning blue. Clay noticed the change as he walked toward the house. The morning was quiet. Allie stayed a few yards away from him. He didn't think it was deliberate, but it was there nonetheless. Each step he took was more difficult. The snow was turning to slush, and his feet were tired. In fact, everything about him felt a little worn down.

Clay wondered suddenly if his father had ever lied and confessed to something he hadn't done. Maybe to keep his mother happy. Living by the truth sometimes didn't seem worth what it cost a man. He and Allie had no chance. That moment in the barn had just proved it. How could he love a woman who thought he would lie about something important enough that her brother had almost been killed? And how could she love him when she thought he had done it?

Allie had been walking a little faster than he had, and he saw her take the few steps onto the porch leading to the door by herself. Clay hadn't seen the front of the house clearly earlier. Now, he noticed the beige siding needed a coat of paint. These harsh winters were to blame, he knew. But when he'd lived on the ranch, everything was kept in perfect condition. It was like the Nelsons had just given up.

All of those years when he had been serving his time, Clay had known that things would change on the ranch after the night of the robbery. He'd expected Mr. Nelson would be testier than usual. And that Allie would be sad. But he'd never expected the neglect that he'd seen since he'd been back.

Allie stood in the doorway, holding the door open for him, and he stepped through it into the warmth of the kitchen. The rug was there and Clay stood on it, bending to scrape the snow off his boots. Allie did the same.

The smell of bacon still scented the air, but the table had been cleared. The dishes had been washed and were drying on a rack by the sink.

Mr. Nelson walked out of the hallway into the kitchen.

"Good, you're back." He reached for the pocket in his coveralls and pulled out a crumpled piece of gray paper. "I keep forgetting. Mark wrote this. Gave it to me a couple of weeks ago when I saw him."

The rancher held it out to Clay. "It's got your name on it. It's not private or anything. Mark said I could read it."

"Let me get my boots off first," Clay said as he sat down on the bench by the door and took them off. There was no other way to keep from trailing wet snow around the house. Only then did he stand back up.

"Thanks," Clay said as he walked across the floor in his stocking feet and took the paper.

"Jeremy is in the back bedroom talking with that cat of his," Mr. Nelson announced. "Never knew he could jabber so much."

"Is the door closed?" Allie asked him. "So Jeremy can't hear us?"

The older man nodded.

Clay wondered what they were so worried about, but there was no time to ask before Allie started talking again.

"Well, what does it say?" Allie asked Clay like she'd never heard that Mark had left a message.

Clay walked over to the table and sat in one of the chairs before he unfolded the note. It was a lined paper, like those in school tablets. The letters were large and ragged—like a small child would write. But they were legible. Clay read the words aloud. "'Dear Clay, I need your help. My girlfriend won't talk to me. She broke up with me, but I think I can get her back if you help me. Be a good buddy. I think she'd be impressed if I do the wagon for Easter morning. The doctor said I can go if someone drives the thing for me. Remember I told you about that? It's a big deal around here. Her mother makes her go to church on Easter so I know she'll be there. I'll be some kind of hero that day. I'm going to ask her to go to dinner with me after church on Easter. How can she say no? I'll owe you one if you help me.'"

The note was signed "Mark."

There was a postscript. "Your brother—sort of. For real."

Clay was silent after he finished reading the words. He glanced over at Allie. She met his gaze.

"He could have asked me to help," she whispered.

She had her boots off, too, and walked over to sit in a chair at the table, as well.

"I would do anything for him," she added.

Clay felt relieved that she sat down beside

him. But he shook his head slowly. "It's a guy thing. He can't ask his little sister to help get his girlfriend back. Besides, you used to tease him mercilessly about him dating someone."

Allie scowled at him, but she couldn't seem to stop her lips from curving up in a smile. "Well, he was too busy for all that. He wanted to go to college and he almost had that scholarship." She thought a moment. "He still has the scholarship, I think. They froze it for him in case—"

Clay wondered if he should feel so good just to be talking with her.

"He did have plans, didn't he?" Clay said, hoping to lighten her emotions. When he first heard about that scholarship, Clay remembered wondering how Mark could bear to leave the ranch. But he was set on college and then medical school. It was Allie who wanted to stay and work with the horses. Now it was questionable whether either one of them would have their dreams.

Mr. Nelson was still standing in the doorway, clearly lost in his own memories. "When he was a little boy, Mark always liked to get up at five o'clock on Easter morning and drive our old hay wagon down the street, leading everyone to that seven o'clock service behind the church. I used to let him sit on my lap and take the reins. People would just stand outside there and look up at the old cross. Mark was a good boy. And he loved Easter. Called it the best day of the year. I should have seen it coming, but I didn't know he realized the time of year. They don't give him a calendar. He wouldn't have known when Easter was coming, either, except last month he saw some decorations in the nurse's station and asked when the day was. He wanted me to tell Clay to get the wagon ready. You know people around here count on that tradition. That and the yellow daffodils—they make Easter morning."

"He still doesn't need Clay," Allie said quietly.

"He seems to think he does," Mr. Nelson replied. "He said Clay agreed to help him."

Mr. Nelson finally walked over and sat at the table also.

"I will do what I can," Clay told him. "But I haven't heard from him." The prison was pretty good about getting mail to the inmates, and he had heard regularly from Mrs. Hargrove. "Did he write and ask me to help with that? Maybe he expected you to mail the note he wrote." The older man shook his head. "Well, Mark and Hannah must have been off and on for some time now."

Mr. Nelson was silent for a minute longer.

He studied the floor, seeming to be searching for an answer, and then looked up to meet his daughter's gaze.

"We have to tell him everything," Mr. Nelson finally said to Allie. "It won't make sense otherwise."

She nodded and looked at Clay, her eyes searching for something in his face. "But you have to keep what we tell you to yourself. We haven't told anyone around here. People know that Mark is improving and getting better every day, but they don't know the full situation. They think he's still just wiggling a few toes."

Allie stopped then as though she couldn't go on, but she kept staring intently at Clay. "You have to promise to keep it a secret—at least until Mark says it's okay to say something. We don't know, but it could hurt him in his recovery if we're not careful. Like ripping off a bandage too soon. That's what the doctors say."

Clay nodded. "I'd never do anything to make his situation worse. I don't lie, but I can keep a secret."

Allie kept her eyes on Clay as though she was still taking his measure. Finally, she spoke. "Mark doesn't know how much time has passed since his accident. He thinks it's just now coming on to Easter. He must have asked you about helping with the Easter wagon that year before the accident."

"He did—" Clay said. "But that was back then."

They had been reading the Gospel of Luke for that challenge at the church. Mark said it would be great fun to bring the cross to the back of the church for the processional.

Clay was beginning to understand.

"Mark only knows what he's told," Allie continued as she paced the kitchen floor. Then she turned to her father. "We need to tell Mark he can't do it. Anybody in the church could say something to him. Surely, they will. And it's too many people to keep a secret. This coming Sunday is Palm Sunday. Then it's Easter. There's not time for Mark to be ready to do something like that."

Mr. Nelson shrugged. "The doctor thinks it will be good for Mark. He's figuring Clay can drive the wagon. People won't even necessarily know Mark is there. We'll have him so wrapped in blankets no one will see him. But Mark is expecting Clay to do this with him, and he wants to see Clay anyway. I'm thinking Clay can leave the wagon and drive Mark home after the service in that old red pickup. Mark won't even need to speak to anyone else."

"But what about Hannah?" Clay asked. "Is she on board? She's the one Mark wants to talk to. He's not going to be happy to make all of this effort if she isn't even there on Easter morning."

"Mark might do it for the church anyway," Allie said, but she didn't look convinced.

"Trust me, he'll want her to be there," Clay said. No wonder Mark asked him to help with this. Any guy would know what was important.

Mr. Nelson looked uncomfortable, and Allie didn't say anymore.

"She—ah—" Mr. Nelson stuttered. "Hannah's moved on with her life. I'm afraid she's given up on Mark. She hasn't been to see him since he's been regaining consciousness. She came a few times early on, but—"

Mr. Nelson let his words taper off.

"She might have come without us knowing," Allie interjected.

Clay recognized that look. She wasn't convinced.

"You want to think she would have come," Clay corrected Allie. She always saw the best in everyone. Well, except for him, Clay told himself.

Allie nodded.

"And he wants me to get her interested in

him?" Clay asked. It suddenly hit him how big the problem was. "He doesn't know four years have passed since that night. Is that right?"

"He doesn't remember anything after Hannah broke up with him," Allie said. "Not even the robbery. Or where the two of you got that tequila."

Her father winced as he stood there. "The alcohol isn't important. You need to forget about that. It doesn't matter where they got that tequila."

"Nothing about the robbery?" Clay asked. "He's forgotten all that?"

"That's right," the older man said. "His mind is wiped clean of the memory. And the doctor said we shouldn't force Mark to remember. He needs to do it in his time."

"But he will remember?" Clay asked.

"We don't know," Mr. Nelson said. "He hasn't so far."

Clay let the words settle in. He hadn't even let himself hope yet that Mark would one day be able to set the record straight on that night. Now it appeared that it might not happen. Mark was the only other person who knew the truth. Clay realized for the first time that he likely would never be acknowledged as innocent. Allie would never know the truth of what happened.

"I'll do whatever I can to help," Clay said firmly. Now was not the time to worry about himself. Mark needed his help. "I can't make any guarantees about Hannah, though. I don't have much experience with women."

Allie lifted one eyebrow and smirked.

"What?" Clay remembered her wearing that same expression when her brother said something outrageous. She'd never given Clay that look before. "I told you before I didn't."

Her eyes were shaded and her voice smooth. "Don't expect me to believe that."

She'd never used that tone with Mark, either. There was nothing girlish about the sound. It was warm and feminine.

Clay's heart started beating faster, but his tongue was tied up in knots. What a tangle they were in. He could see Allie didn't like thinking of him with other women. He wondered where she thought he'd gotten any experience dating anyway. But she didn't like it. Allie's voice had almost sounded like she was flirting with him.

He must be hallucinating, he told himself. He thought she'd never warm to him.

The sound of the clock ticking was all that filled the silence. Allie thought it should be soothing, but it made her edgy. Her breath kept coming fast. She couldn't take her eyes off Clay. He seemed a little stunned as well, his blue eyes wary. The sun coming in the window at them showed the dark stubble on his face. She didn't want to keep staring, so she turned her head slightly. That's when she saw her father studying her like he was trying to puzzle something out. The last person in the world she wanted speculating about her feelings toward Clay was her father. When he caught her eye, though, he spoke.

"You still trying to figure out where that tequila came from?" he asked, his head tipped to one side.

Allie blinked. So that was what he was thinking about.

"You can't buy tequila in Dry Creek," Allie said. "I'm sure there are a few places in Miles City that carry it, but there's no need for you to concern yourself with it. Mark wouldn't have bought any tequila that night."

Allie knew her father was an alcoholic. Even if he had stopped drinking before her mother died, he still fixated on anything to do with alcohol. At least, Allie certainly hoped that was it and that he hadn't been trying to find a place to buy some alcohol.

The sound of an engine coming up their drive distracted everyone.

"That'll be Randy," Allie said. "One of you go meet him and I'll get dinner ready. We need to fix the corral fence first so the horses have room to move."

"I'll go out with Jeremy and check the chickens, too," her father said. "There won't be any eggs today, but I thought he'd like to know where the nests are."

"I'll take Randy to the bunkhouse," Clay offered. "That is, if he wants to stay tonight."

"It's up to him," Allie said as she walked over to the kitchen cabinets. "We'll only need his help for a few days, though, so he might not want to move anything out here."

Within minutes, Allie was alone in the kitchen. She had already put a roast in the oven, but she'd need to peel some potatoes and put together a salad. Before she started in with the food, though, there was something she had to do.

She opened all of the cabinets and took a slow look at what she could see. Then she got a step stool and stood closer to the shelves, moving the spice bottles and flour sacks to the side. Her mother had told her that she needed to do more than check behind the tall containers like those for vinegar or molasses. A bottle of alcohol, she'd said, could be placed on its side and hidden behind short items, too.

Allie didn't expect to find anything, but she routinely checked every time she came home. She did it for her mother, who had told Allie that her father always hid his bottles in the kitchen cabinets.

Five minutes later, Allie found the bottle behind her mother's prized blue willow plates in one of the bottom cupboards. From the looks of the faded label, the bottle was likely from before her father had given up drinking. The cork hadn't been secure and a dark stain marked where the last of the bourbon had leaked out years ago. She gently lifted the bottle, knowing from the light weight that it was empty.

Both her parents had always said her father drank only whiskey. She realized then that if her father had been drinking bourbon back in those days, he might also have bought a bottle of tequila.

Allie carefully took all of the blue willow plates off their shelf. As she was growing up, they used these dishes only for holidays or sometimes Sunday dinners. In spite of everything, she smiled as she brought those dishes out. When she washed them as a girl, her mother would explain that the picture of the willow trees and bridge showed the tragic story of a young Chinese woman and the man she loved.

Allie had been enthralled with the story plates, as she called them, wondering at the strong love that would make the young couple risk their lives in hopes of being together.

Allie shook her head. She wondered if she'd have the courage to really love someone like that. To her, everything seemed murky. She wondered if she was right to ignore the tugging in her heart for Clay. He demanded she believe him; she refused to ignore what seemed to be true. They had less hope of being together than that poor Chinese couple on the plates.

After she had potatoes boiling and sourdough rolls heating in the oven, Allie washed the blue willow dishes and dried them. She told herself it was foolish to put them away without using them, so she set them on the table.

The kitchen was quiet. The sun was high in the sky, and the day was warm. She glanced out the window and saw a single set of footprints in the melting snow leading all the way to the barn. The footprints were disappearing into puddles.

Then she saw the barn door open. Allie watched as Jeremy stepped in Clay's larger footprints, even though the snow had mostly gone. She had done the same when she was a little girl walking behind her father.

She remembered then that there was a jar of homemade apple butter somewhere in the cupboard, and after she set some honey on the table, Allie turned back to look for it. She didn't know if Jeremy had ever had apple butter, but she knew Clay hadn't tasted it before coming to the ranch.

By the time she had drained the potatoes, Clay, Randy, her father and Jeremy had come inside.

"What's the occasion?" her father asked when he saw the table.

"I was looking down in the cupboards and saw mom's special dishes," Allie said. "Decided I might as well wash them and use them when we eat."

Allie watched her father's face as he unwound the scarf from around his neck. One moment his face was relaxed, and the next, he'd gone pale. She saw the guilty look he gave the bottom cupboard. He didn't say anything, but she noticed he was trying to figure out what to do.

"I found it," Allie said then.

Her father's shoulders slumped. "I forgot it was there."

"Since when did you drink bourbon?" she asked, her voice tight.

He didn't answer right away, but he finally

started. "After your mother died, there were a couple of years when I was drinking anything I could get my hands on, and a bar in Miles City was going out of business. They had a sale, and I bought a few bottles real cheap."

Allie smelled the roasted beef. Everything was dished up. The mashed potatoes. The gravy. The bread was ready to take from the oven. A bowl of green peas stood on the sideboard. But she had no appetite. She wondered if any of the men did, either. Clay was looking at her like he was trying to figure out what was wrong. Randy had a slight frown on his face. Jeremy was looking at the adults as though he knew something was amiss.

Allie turned to her father. "Was one of those bottles tequila?"

He was silent for a long moment. "I never liked the stuff."

Allie knew what that meant. "So the bottle was almost full when Mark found it."

It wasn't Clay who had given Mark the alcohol, Allie realized.

"I'm sorry I didn't believe you when you said that the bottle wasn't yours," she said to Clay. She felt ashamed. "I will do what I can to set the record straight."

"How would you do that?" Clay asked quietly.

"If you're still going to say something in church tomorrow, I'll stand by you on the question of where the alcohol came from," Allie said.

Her father made a sound of protest, but when she looked over at him, he shook his head. "I'm sorry. I didn't want to admit I still had a problem with alcohol. I'd promised your mother I was giving the stuff up and then—"

"I don't need to mention the alcohol tomorrow," Clay said. "And Randy won't say anything, will you?"

The ranch hand shook his head. "That's right. I won't."

Allie looked at Clay incredulously. "I thought that the whole point of saying something tomorrow is that you want people to believe you. This is your chance."

"Having your father confess about the alcohol won't make anyone believe I had nothing to do with the robbery," Clay said.

Allie wondered if Clay meant she wouldn't believe it, but she wasn't going to ask. She had been hoping it would be enough for him if she agreed with him that he hadn't provided the alcohol. She saw now that it wouldn't be enough for either one of them. But she couldn't wear blinders, no matter how much she wished for it to be true that Clay was innocent.

"Isn't it enough if you are just forgiven?" she asked him. "The church will do that much."

He didn't answer her, but she could see from the faces of all the men that forgiveness wasn't enough for a proud man.

"We may as well eat then," she said.

Clay helped her put the food on the table like he had done for breakfast, but he didn't talk, and when it came time to say the blessing for the meal, no one held hands.

Father, forgive us, Allie added silently to her father's prayer. *Help us to understand each other.* She looked across the table at Clay. *And accept each other.*

Chapter Nine

The sun rose bright the next morning, the light shining through the blinds. Clay opened his eyes a little and squinted. The linoleum on the floor was cold, and he felt his hand resting against it. He was puzzled a moment and then remembered he was in the bunkhouse. He'd moved the mattress from his bunk bed to the kitchen floor in the middle of the night because Randy snored. Which probably wasn't the real problem, Clay told himself. He'd listened to dozens of men snoring at night in prison and it hadn't stopped him from sleeping. No, what kept Clay awake was that Randy talked in his sleep.

Clay groaned as he rolled over so he could see the small clock he'd plugged in last night. It was a little before six o'clock. Church was at ten o'clock, and there were chores to do before he got ready.

He had asked Allie for a box of cold cereal last night, and she'd given him that and a small carton of milk. He didn't want her to have to get up early on Sunday morning to cook him and Randy breakfast.

Clay heard a noise by the doorway and looked over to see Randy. The ranch hand was wrapped in a blanket, and his hair looked like he'd spent the night wrestling with someone.

"Who is Lois?" Clay asked as he lay there.

Randy glared. "What do you mean?"

"You were talking about her last night in your sleep," Clay said with a yawn. "I thought she might be someone special. You know, your mother or someone."

"Lois isn't my mother," Randy snapped.

"Well, then—" Clay started to continue.

"She's none of your business," Randy said then, with enough fire in his voice that Clay decided she was someone important.

"Sorry," Clay murmured. "I won't mention her again."

"See that you don't," Randy said as he walked over to the refrigerator. "Did you get us orange juice?"

"Milk and cold cereal," Clay said as he sat up on the mattress. "That's all."

Randy grunted at that news and stomped back into the other room.

Clay decided it was a poor morning when he and Randy Collins had nothing better to do than feel sorry for themselves, but that's the kind of day it was shaping up to be.

"We need to get some more wood to build another fire," Randy called from the other room. "We could freeze to death in here. Besides, we'll want hot water for when we shave."

"It's not that cold," Clay said as he stood up. They'd had a fire last night, and the water from the tap was warm. He kept a blanket around him and thought he was doing pretty well until he put his feet on the freezing floor.

"I'll get some wood in a minute," he called out to Randy. "You get some of the kindling going."

Clay opened the back door just enough to pull in some logs. Fortunately, they were dry since it hadn't snowed last night.

"I'll heat a pot of water on the stove for shaving," Clay called out, as well.

It wouldn't be the first time Clay had gone to church with a dark shadow from not shaving, but he figured it was best that he look as sharp as he could this morning. People were sure to take a good look at the ex-con who was out on parole. He didn't want to give them any reason to doubt the account he was going to give of the robbery.

"You're welcome to use my aftershave," Randy called. "It's on the shelf in the bathroom. Sort of pine smelling."

"Thanks," Clay called back. He couldn't remember Randy ever offering to share something with him, and it felt good. Maybe the other man knew it would be hard for Clay to walk into the sanctuary this morning wearing old jeans and a shirt that was frayed around the bottom.

"I'll give you a ride to church, if you want," Clay offered in return. "Mr. Nelson told me I could use the red pickup."

As he got dressed, Clay mused on how people were basically good. Randy might be a little testy when talking about his Lois, but he was all right. They'd cleaned the bunkhouse yesterday afternoon, and Randy had accepted the Nelsons' invitation to stay a few nights.

Clay fed the horses while Randy tended to the chickens and the pig. They both ended up feeding the goat. Mostly because the animal was unpredictable. It took one man to feed him and another to be sure the goat behaved. Everyone was fed and watered, though, by a little before nine o'clock, which left both men time to polish their shoes and be ready to leave for church on time. Clay put the sheepskin coat on. If he kept that on, no one would notice his clothes. And, he had to admit that he smelled good with that pine aftershave of Randy's.

"People are going to think we're a forest," Clay said as he and Randy gathered up their things for church.

"Better that we smell of forest than of old goat," Randy said with a grin.

Clay answered with a chuckle. He patted the pocket of his coat where he still had about twenty dollars. He'd like to put something in the offering plate just to prove that he could. At the last minute he went to the shelf in the kitchen and picked up the old Bible sitting there. He'd take that, too.

Clay heard the door to the main house open. Mr. Nelson, Allie and the boy were heading out, and he knew that meant it was time for him and Randy to get going, as well.

"This old thing gets around," Randy said as he climbed into the passenger seat of the pickup. "Remember when we used to load it with a few bales of hay and take it out to the horses?"

Clay nodded. "Those were the good old days."

He got inside and put the key in the ignition. "The heater doesn't work very well."

"It's okay," Randy said.

Clay studied the fields as he drove down the gravel road. When he'd come in earlier, it was all dark. But now he could see the gray dirt showing through patches of melting snow. Brown tufts of weeds and rocks were sprinkled over the land.

Clay passed several pickups heading into Dry Creek.

"What's up with the traffic?" he asked Randy.

The other man shrugged. "Guess word is out that you're going to speak."

Clay gasped and turned to him in shock. "I'm just going to make a small announcement during prayer time. Did you tell everyone I was going to speak?"

"Watch the road," Randy said when Clay stared at him.

Clay's hands tightened on the steering wheel as he turned back. Then he slowed the pickup. They were past the café and the hardware store.

"Well, people want to hear it, whatever it is." Randy's voice was confident. "I've heard them talking."

"Where?" Clay looked over at the ranch hand. "I just got back here. No one even knows I'm here."

Randy snorted at that. "You woke half the town up driving through it yesterday morning. It didn't take much for them to tell the other half of the town that you'd come back."

Clay wished he'd stayed home. Or, well, at the bunkhouse. It was too late, of course, to go back. He'd already pulled the pickup to a stop on the side of the road next to the church. A woman in a hat had smiled at him. And he saw Mrs. Hargrove climbing the center stairs with her husband, Charley.

"They have pretty good coffee inside," Randy said as though he could tell Clay was reluctant to keep going. "Sometimes doughnuts, too."

Clay figured he was trapped, so he reached over and opened the door of the pickup. There was a strong wind as he stepped down, and he reached up to keep his hat in place. When he looked back at the church, he saw Allie and Jeremy walking up the steps. Allie was wearing a gray wool coat, and the wind was swirling two tails of a long bright scarf around her neck. Red was mixing with gold and orange. Allie's hair was uncovered, and strands of it flew with the scarf. She held Jeremy by the hand, and the boy squealed with pleasure in the wind.

Clay sensed someone standing beside him and looked over to see Randy staring, too.

"Who would have thought," the ranch hand said. "She used to be a scruffy-looking tomboy."

"She was always beautiful," Clay said quietly as he started to walk toward the church.

Randy grunted as he followed. "By the way, that's the other foster kid over there."

Randy gestured with his head, and Clay saw the teenager standing by a pickup on the other side of the church. The youngster was dressed in a black hoodie and jeans. Most of the teenage boys around Dry Creek wore plaid shirts and blue jeans, so Clay figured the boy was proving he was different. Or maybe that's all he had. Clay recognized the vehicle as belonging to the Redfern ranch, so he guessed not as much had changed around here as he thought. The men who worked there used that old blue thing to feed the hay in the winter and come to church on Sundays.

Clay saw the boy watching him, so he wondered if he knew who Clay was.

"Hi, there," Clay called to him with a nod of the head.

Clay got a glare in response. That's when he noticed the nose ring on the teenager. The kid shifted his legs then, and Clay saw a crease in his jeans near his right ankle. The boy had a knife sheath snug to his calf. Whether it was empty or not, Clay couldn't tell.

"What's his name?" Clay asked Randy quietly so that the boy wouldn't hear.

"Henry," Randy said as he started taking the steps up to the church. "They call him Hen for short."

Clay kept his head down until they both stepped into the entry to the sanctuary. The sound of the wind was cut off suddenly, and the air was warm inside. He wasn't sure, but he thought the sounds of people talking quieted considerably while he stood there. About half of the people were making their way to the pews, and the other half were standing by the coat racks.

The church looked the same as he remembered. A polished mahogany cross hung from the front of the room. A row of square windows, filled with stained glass, went down both sides of the church. Two rows of pews, with a carpeted pathway, went down the length of the sanctuary. A wood pulpit stood on a slight rise in the front.

He recognized many of the faces, but he had a hard time thinking of the matching names. Most of the women wore dark slacks and sweaters. The men wore cotton shirts and ties. No one wore a suit.

He saw Allie's bright scarf out of the side of one eye and turned his head. Mr. Nelson, Allie and Jeremy were settling into one of the pews on the right side. Allie had her head bent down, talking with Jeremy, and the next thing he noticed the boy was slipping out of the pew and walking toward him.

"Aunt Allie said you was to come sit with us," Jeremy whispered as he put a hand out to Clay. Then he reached the other hand out to Randy.

Clay looked at Allie, but she was facing toward the front and didn't even see him. He wondered if Allie had really made the invitation or if Jeremy just wanted some company.

Randy shrugged and started allowing the boy to lead him, so Clay did the same. No one seemed to think anything was unusual as Jeremy guided Clay into the pew, not even when Clay ended up sitting next to Allie.

Clay saw a pink flush on Allie's face as he looked over at her. She must be embarrassed. Then he remembered what a small-town church was like. The people there probably all thought that he and Allie had some kind of understanding.

The thought settled well with him.

"Morning," he whispered as he leaned over slightly.

Allie smiled back.

Mrs. Hargrove started playing the piano, and the few stragglers hurried to find seats. By the time the older woman had finished the song, the pastor was behind the pulpit and ready with a hymn for them all to sing.

The last chords had scarcely faded away when the pastor asked Charley Nelson to come up to the pulpit and give the announcements. "We have a special guest with us today," Charley began, looking every inch an old-time rancher, with his white shirt accented by a silver bolo tie and his worn jeans sporting a silver belt buckle.

Clay's arm brushed against Allie and he could feel her tense up as Charley spoke.

"Clay West wants to say a few words to us," Charley said as he stepped away from the pulpit to make room for him.

"I'll pray for you," Allie whispered as Clay stood up.

He looked down at her and nodded. He supposed it would make her feel better to pray. Then he made his way past Jeremy and Randy and walked to the front.

Clay stood behind the pulpit and swallowed. He looked around. He saw Sheriff Wall sitting there with his wife and kids. The man had a good poker face. Clay couldn't tell what he thought. He saw Mrs. Hargrove in her usual seat close to the piano. She was beaming at him, but then she had experience encouraging nervous speakers given all the kindergarteners she'd helped say their lines at Christmas pageants.

He saw some of the wranglers from the Elkton ranch and Mr. and Mrs. Redfern. He slowly looked from face to face, seeing curiosity in most of them and condemnation in a few.

"I suppose you know my story," Clay began. "I've been in prison for four years now, and Mr. Nelson has helped set me up with a parole. I thank him for that. It's important to me that you know I didn't plan that robbery, though. I don't steal. I don't lie." Clay didn't want to talk about Mark's part in that night, so he found he didn't have much more to say. "Since I'm going to be around here, I wanted you to know. That's all."

Clay didn't even need to see the faces out in the pews. He could almost feel their shock. Jaws were slack, and he could hear whispers. Maybe he had been too outspoken. He did notice a couple of the older men glaring at him.

"We forgive you," one of the women in the front row called out. Clay couldn't remember her name, but he saw a few heads nodding in relief. The older men weren't among them, though.

"I don't need your forgiveness," Clay said and walked back down the aisle.

He didn't get to the door before Charley had regained the pulpit and called out, "Wait."

Clay turned to look at the other man.

"I need to make the announcement for the Easter sunrise service," Charley said, his eyes trained on Clay. "We'll meet at the edge of town by the stop sign at seven o'clock and form a processional to the area behind the church. My wife tells me our daffodils should be in full bloom by then. We'll keep the tarps on until that Sunday. The weather looks like we'll have some cold snaps, but they're set to bloom like always. God is faithful to us."

Charley paused, and Clay figured the announcement was over. He turned to finish his walk to the door when Charley spoke again.

"We're hoping you will help with the processional," Charley said, still looking directly at Clay. "As a tribute to your friend Mark Nelson."

Clay felt firmly caught. He wondered if Charley knew that Mr. Nelson had already asked him to do just that. Whether he had or not, there could be only one answer.

"I'll do it," Clay said, his voice heavy.

Mr. Nelson stood up then from where he sat in the pew. "Mark is going to be there, too. Clay is going to make that happen."

A rush of exclamations greeted that news along with a few hands clapping. This announcement was something they understood.

Clay saw the concerned look on Allie's face. She had wanted to keep Mark's presence quiet. But there was no way to unsay those words.

Clay needed to escape into the fresh air. He was done for now. He opened the door and stepped outside onto the cement steps. He felt like he could finally breathe again as he leaned back against the doors. He noticed then that the two doors didn't meet well in the middle.

From where Clay stood, he could still hear the voice of the pastor asking everyone to open their Bibles to the Gospel of Luke. They were going to talk about Palm Sunday, he said, and what it meant to have faith.

Clay looked straight ahead and saw Hen, the foster kid, sitting in the Redfern pickup with a knowing smirk on his face.

Clay had planned to go and sit in the pickup until the sermon was over, but he didn't want to set a bad example for that kid. At least that's what he told himself as he found himself standing by the door.

Clay figured maybe the kid would come up and listen with him, but he didn't. Eventually, Clay forgot about anyone else as he concentrated on the words. After the pastor finished, Clay decided he'd go home tonight and read the whole Gospel of Luke just as he and Mark had set out to do four years ago.

Clay had barely managed to make it down the steps before the doors to the church were thrown open and Jeremy raced down them, as well.

"We're staying for dinner," the boy announced joyfully when he got to the bottom and stared up at Clay. "Mrs. Hargrove invited us. She's making tamales."

"Is that right?" Clay asked as he knelt down to Jeremy's height. The boy was jumping around in excitement. "Have you ever eaten a tamale?"

The boy nodded vigorously and then turned to point up the stairs. "Auntie will tell you."

Clay looked up and saw Allie standing at the top of the steps. Her coat was open, flapping slightly in the wind. Her head was bowed so she could see him, and she looked dismayed.

Clay stood back up. He didn't want to upset anyone. Things here in Dry Creek weren't what he expected, though. He wondered if he'd been too quick to judge people before. Maybe they hadn't been as set against him as he had thought.

Allie caught her breath. Clay looked like he was trying for a quick getaway when Jeremy had caught him. She had no idea what he was planning to do now. She noticed Clay was smiling at her nephew, though.

"Mrs. Hargrove gets her tamales from the sheriff's wife," Allie said. "They are really very good. Chicken and beef ones. And some special spicy ones she ordered with you in mind."

"I like hot food," Clay said.

Allie nodded. "Mrs. Hargrove knows. Extra chili peppers."

Clay smiled, and she watched his face transform itself. He appeared years younger, the way he used to look years ago when they had a new colt born on the place and he'd been happy.

Allie heard the door open behind her, and she turned to see who else was leaving the church before the coffee was served. It was Mrs. Hargrove. The older woman stepped to the far right on the stairs so that she could grab the handrail. She carefully started to step down, and Allie rushed over to take her other arm. Fortunately, the short piece of walkway in front of the church and the whole stairway were always shoveled off before services. So by now, the steps were free of ice and they were dry.

When Allie and the older woman reached the bottom of the stairs, Mrs. Hargrove held out her arms, and Clay stepped into them eagerly. Allie watched the two of them hug each other tight. They made a strange sight, a white-haired farm woman and a young man with a prison haircut, but there was no doubt of their affection for each other.

She heard Mrs. Hargrove repeatedly whisper, "Welcome home."

Allie was stricken with remorse as she contrasted Mrs. Hargrove's greeting with the one Clay had received at the Nelson ranch. Maybe guilt and judgment weren't as important as love and forgiveness. Her only saving grace, Allie thought, was that no one else in Dry Creek had idolized Clay like she had. He had further to fall in her estimate than in anyone else's.

Still, she wished she had welcomed him home.

Chapter Ten

A little while later, Allie was in Mrs. Hargrove's kitchen and the other woman was taking a pan of Spanish rice out of the oven. The air was warm and smelled of cooked beef. Wide windows on the left of the room looked out to the yard. A small wooden table stood next to old-fashioned white cabinets. A bowl of lettuce salad sat on the counter, bright red tomatoes and green cucumbers peeking out between the leaves. A small meat loaf sat cooling on one of the stove burners. A huge platter of tamales sat on another burner.

"There's ice in the top freezer to fill the glasses," Mr. Hargrove said as she moved around the kitchen. She wore a large ivory apron with large pockets that covered most of her green-checked gingham housedress. She'd changed after she came in the door after church, saying she didn't want to get any spots on her new wool suit.

It was the suit more than anything that told Allie the older woman saw this as an important day. Most of Mrs. Hargrove's Sunday clothes were simple polyester dresses in navy or gray. The wool suit was a beautiful pale pink with dark rose piping around the edge of the collar.

"You looked particularly nice this morning," Allie said as she reached into the freezer and pulled out a tray of ice cubes.

"I ordered the suit from a catalog," the older woman said as she stopped with a small frown on her face. "My daughter, Doris June, suggested it. You don't think it looks too…" She spread her hands as though she couldn't find the word she wanted.

"It was perfect." Allie used a plastic tong to put ice cubes in the dinner glasses.

Mrs. Hargrove nodded in relief, the tight gray curls on her head bouncing as she moved her head. "It's not every day that Clay West comes back home."

Clay and the other men were out in the garage looking at a small saddle Charley had stored from the days when his son was Jeremy's age.

Allie stopped what she was doing. "You think Clay's innocent then?"

Mrs. Hargrove did not answer right away. She was scooping some cooked corn into a serving bowl.

Allie had turned back to the drinks when the older woman answered.

"I'm not sure it matters anymore if Clay is guilty or not," Mrs. Hargrove said. "He served time in prison. He's a good man. You only have to look him in the eyes to know that he's going to try hard to live a worthwhile life. Anyone can make a mistake."

"It seems to matter to him if people think he's innocent or not," Allie said.

The other woman nodded. "Men can be that way. I'm reminded of the Prodigal Son. All the father wanted to do when his son came back was celebrate. Sometimes people forget that with God, guilt isn't permanent. Forgiveness can make us new."

Allie hoped that would be enough for Clay. And for her.

The sound of the door opening in the living room was followed by the thump of many boots.

"They're back," Mrs. Hargrove said as she picked up the platter of tamales. "They'll be ready to eat."

By now, Allie had a tray of ice-filled glasses,

and she lifted it so she could follow Mrs. Hargrove into the dining room.

Sunshine filled the dining room. White net curtains hung at the wide windows along the side of the large wood dining table. A couple of ferns hung from hooks in the tall sills of the windows.

"Auntie, Auntie." Allie heard Jeremy's call before she saw him come running into the dining room.

"Unka Clay is teachin' me ta ride a horse," the boy almost shouted, he was so excited.

Allie almost dropped one of the glasses. She set the glass down on the table before she walked over to her nephew.

By that time, the men had come into the dining room, too. They all had sheepish looks on their faces.

"I made a mistake," Clay confessed. He still had his Stetson and his coat on, so Allie figured he'd only managed to scrape the snow off his boots. "It's all my fault."

"Jeremy," Mrs. Hargrove called. "Why don't you come in the kitchen with me and see if we can find you a cookie. Do you like cookies?"

"Yes, ma'am," the boy said with a grin, happily following the older woman into the other room.

"Now, it wasn't all Clay's fault," Allie's father said to her when the kitchen door was closed.

Charley and Randy stood there looking uncomfortable, but they were quiet.

"We were looking at that saddle Charley's son used when he was a little tyke," Clay began. His eyes met hers, but they were stormy with distress. "Jeremy was all excited about learning to ride a horse and I forgot—I said his father would be pleased that he wanted to ride."

Allie's jaw dropped open.

"We never mention his father," she whispered.

"I know," Clay said. "That's why I said I meant his uncle. His uncle would be pleased. He seemed to accept that. Then he wanted to know who his uncle was. Then—"

Clay turned to look at her father, and Allie followed his gaze.

"Don't look at me," her father said. "Jeremy already knows I'm his grandpa. I can't be his uncle, too. He's a bright boy. He'd figure that one out. So I'm the one who told him Clay was his uncle."

Allie shook her head. "I can't believe this."

"Well, it's sort of true," her father explained. "Clay was a foster son in our family and Mark looks to him as a brother. Clay's the closest thing to an uncle that the boy has. His mother is an only child, and you're a girl."

"Okay," Allie said as she nodded. "I guess I can see that."

"A fatherless boy needs an uncle," her father said.

"In some villages in Africa, an uncle can be nothing more than a family friend," Clay said. "It's an honorary title. I'd like to think I'm that at least."

Allie met Clay's eyes. His hat shaded his face, but she could see he was sincere and nervous. Suddenly, he seemed to remember his Stetson, and he swept it off his head, leaving his hair a little mussed.

"You're going to have to keep your promises to Jeremy," Allie said fiercely. She wasn't so sure it mattered who the boy's uncle was as long as the man was dependable. "I won't stand by and let you disappoint him."

"I never lie," Clay said calmly.

"He's too young to ride a horse," Allie said.

Clay looked at Randy then.

"I figure we'll start him on the goat," Clay confessed. "We've already explained that there will be a training period before he actually sits on a real horse."

Allie was silent as she looked at the men.

"We figured it was the goat or the pig,"

Randy said then, his voice hesitant. "And that pig is too small."

Suddenly, Allie started to giggle.

"Those poor animals have no idea what they are getting into," Allie finally managed to say. By now, everyone was chuckling.

"The boy will do fine," Charley said then. "My pa taught me how to ride on a sawhorse in the barn. A ranch boy has to be flexible. I've heard of small boys learning to ride on large calves."

Mrs. Hargrove opened the kitchen door and stuck her head back into the dining room. "All clear?"

"We're ready to eat," Charley said as he motioned everyone to have a seat.

Allie walked back to the kitchen to help Mrs. Hargrove bring the rest of the food to the table. She was surprised at how relaxed she felt today.

By the time they all were ready to push their chairs back from the table, Clay was full.

"That's the best meal I've had in ages," Clay said to Mrs. Hargrove. "I can't thank you enough. Are you sure I can't chop you some wood before we leave?"

"Absolutely not," the older woman said. Her

face pinked in pleasure. "This is your welcome-home party. You're the guest of honor."

Clay blinked away a sudden tear. This woman had stood by him all the years he'd been away, and it touched him. Fortunately, no one seemed to notice his sudden need to blink.

"I have something to show you," Mrs. Hargrove said then as she slid her chair back from the table. "The dishes can wait."

"I'm more than happy to take care of those dishes for you," Charley said as he pushed his chair back, too. "I figure me and Jeremy can manage to wash everything up fine. How about that, pardner?"

Jeremy nodded his head vigorously.

"I'll give you a hand, too," Randy said as he rose with them.

Clay looked up at the ranch hand in surprise.

"What?" Randy said with a grin. "It's not like I'm wearing an apron or anything."

"Still," Clay muttered. The whole world was shifting. "You have something in the kitchen? A cake or something?"

Mrs. Hargrove chuckled. "It's peach pie, and we're going to serve it after the dishes are done. But before anyone leaves the table, I have an announcement for you."

The older woman reached into the big

pocket in her apron and pulled out a glossy flier and a newspaper article. The flier was folded into thirds, and she held it up like it was something special. The article stayed in her other hand.

"I suppose you're wondering about the artwork you sent me over the years," Mrs. Hargrove said, with a smile for Clay.

"It was just a few sketches," Clay said.

The older woman nodded. "I usually have them hanging on the walls around the dining room. Your agent contacted me, though, and we talked. He was looking for sketches he could enter for an art showing at the Charlie Russell museum in Great Falls."

Clay swallowed back an exclamation of surprise.

"I gave him what he is calling the Dry Creek collection," Mrs. Hargrove continued. "The showing was last week and this—" she waved the newspaper article "—is the review. The art critics are saying you have a bold new look. They call you the next major Western artist."

Clay was speechless. He looked around and saw that everyone at the table seemed at a loss for words, as well.

"That's nice," Clay finally managed to say.

Mrs. Hargrove beamed even more. "They

say there were offers for the collection of sketches starting at twenty thousand dollars. That is for the ten sketches."

"You need to sell," Clay advised with a gasp. "Quick, before they change their minds."

"I wouldn't sell those sketches for anything," the older woman said firmly. "They have sentimental value. I did decide to get them insured, though."

"But—" Clay said, and then stopped. His mouth was hanging open, he knew, but he couldn't seem to collect his thoughts enough to close it.

"I did also say I would ask if you have other collections," Mrs. Hargrove continued. "I talked to your agent, and he'll handle the business side of things. I figure you must have other sketches that can be grouped together. Do you have any other sketches with you?"

"In my old suitcase," Clay said. "It's still under my bunk. I checked it last night before I went to bed. I have dozens of sketches of—"

Suddenly, Clay stopped. He blinked and looked around. He was too rattled by Mrs. Hargrove's news to be thinking straight. "They wouldn't work, though."

"Why not?" Charley asked, his tone suggesting Clay was not making the right choice.

"I bet you could get tens of thousands of dollars for something. The time is right."

"They're private sketches," Clay finally said.

"What of?" Mr. Nelson asked. "It didn't seem like you were old enough when you were here to have much that was private."

Everyone looked at Clay as though trying to picture his secrets. He resisted the urge to squirm in his chair. He figured there was no hope of hiding anything. "I drew a few pictures of Allie."

He looked down at the table.

"Was she...?" Randy looked around and whispered, "You know...naked?"

Clay snapped his head back up. "Of course not."

His face was red and he couldn't look over at Allie, although he wanted to know how she was taking all of this.

"Well, what was Allie doing?" Mrs. Hargrove asked then. She, at least, seemed reasonable.

"She was looking out the window," Clay said. "One was her riding her horse. A couple of her with the new colts. One of her all dressed up for church. A few of her in the kitchen."

There was silence as everyone seemed to absorb this.

"You sketched me?" Allie finally asked, her voice one of awe. "I never thought you even noticed me."

"I noticed," Clay said.

"Well, are you willing to give them over to those collectors?" Charley asked. "I think you could get a pretty penny for them."

"It's up to Allie," Clay said, looking at her directly for the first time since the conversation had started.

"I'd be honored," she said.

Clay nodded.

"I'll let that agent of yours know," Mrs. Hargrove said. "He said he could come by Dry Creek tomorrow."

Clay started to agree, and then he remembered. "I'm going to go see Mark tomorrow."

"We can work it out," Mrs. Hargrove said. "Maybe I'll tell him to come Wednesday morning. Would that give you enough time?"

Clay was struck with uncertainty. "The paper I used might have gone bad sitting in that suitcase all these years. I can't promise anything until I see the sketches." He looked at Allie. "You'll have to give me your approval, too, before we close any deals."

Allie nodded.

"What suitcase is that?" Mrs. Hargrove asked.

Clay shrugged. "Just a case that was in the trunk of the car when my parents had their accident all those years ago. It was empty, but the policeman gave it to me days later. I took it to my first foster home and kept it all the way through until I brought it here."

"I remember you had it when you came to the ranch," Allie confirmed.

"It's under my bunk now," Clay added. "Full of this and that from my years bouncing around from place to place. None of it worth anything."

"It's certainly worth something now," Mrs. Hargrove said gently.

Everyone was silent.

"Well, I think that this all calls for peach pie," Mrs. Hargrove finally said. "With ice cream."

Clay sat back in his chair. If it wasn't for the strength of the spindles in the chair, he would be slumped down. He wondered if he was opening a door to something wonderful or something terrifying. It wasn't just the events with the sketches that had surprised him. He was almost as astonished at the ease with which Jeremy had adopted him as his honorary uncle.

He didn't know what more to say about either one of those things. Fortunately, no words were needed because Charley brought in the pie.

Chapter Eleven

Allie was anxious to get home with her father and Jeremy. Clay followed in the pickup while she drove her father's SUV. Randy was spending the afternoon in Dry Creek with his cousin. The snow had melted along the road except for a few small white patches. Gray clouds were gathering in the north, and she realized they might have more snow tonight. Spring wasn't coming to Dry Creek on its regular schedule this year.

She had to admit that it had felt good to drive into the ranch property and see the horses out in the corral. From a distance, no one would know that any of the Appaloosas were blind. Their coats were beautiful in the afternoon sunlight, muscles rippling as they trotted around the enclosure. She wished she had a camera.

Clay stopped the old red pickup next to the parked SUV and stepped out of the driver's door. He walked along the side of the pickup and reached over to pull the small saddle out of the back of the vehicle.

"I'll take this to the tack room," Clay said.

Allie and her father had both doors of the SUV open, and Jeremy climbed out the passenger side.

"My saddle," Jeremy said with pride as he raced over to the pickup.

"It sure is, partner," Clay told the boy.

Allie watched the man and the boy walk through the yard to the barn.

She looked over and saw her father studying them, too. "Not a better man around to teach that boy to ride than Clay West," he said.

Allie nodded. "I always hoped Mark would do it, though."

"I'm not sure Mark will ever be able to ride again," her father said. "He's better, but I just don't know."

Allie reached over and put her hand on her father's arm. "We'll take things day by day."

He grinned. "Mark will be happy if he can just ride in that wagon on Easter morning."

Allie gave a brief nod. "I'm going to go ask Clay to bring those sketches into the kitchen.

Do you really think some collector will pay money for them?"

Her father shrugged. "That's what Mrs. Hargrove says, and she's not one to overstate things."

"You don't think they would sell for more than twenty thousand dollars?" Allie asked in astonishment, but by then her father was already walking up the steps.

He turned back when he got to the door, though. "You should read the article in that art magazine. They sure thought Clay's sketches were something. Said he had expressive lines—whatever that means."

Allie walked over to the barn and stood in the open door. She had dress boots on, so she didn't have to be too cautious with the soles, although she didn't want to do them any damage. She didn't mind standing in the doorway, though. She could hear Jeremy chatting in the tack room and smiled. He usually took a long time to warm up to strangers, but he liked Clay.

Clay stepped out of the room where the saddles were stored, and Allie felt her heart skip a beat. The sun streamed in behind him from the high window in the room. His hat was tipped back enough that she could see the smile around his eyes.

"We got Jeremy's saddle hung up," Clay announced as he started walking toward the door. Her nephew marched along beside him.

"I figure we can take a lesson after nap time," Clay added.

Jeremy looked up as though he was going to protest, but he didn't.

"Cowboys need their sleep," Clay announced.

Allie grinned. She had never gotten Jeremy to agree to lie down and sleep a bit in the afternoon, not even when she knew he took naps when he was home with his mother.

"We might as well throw in a glass of milk while we're at it," Allie said as the man and boy came closer.

Clay winked at her. "I explained that riding a horse is a privilege and requires some extra preparation like naps and doing chores."

"You'll make a good…uncle," Allie stumbled. She'd been about to say *father*. She'd never thought that about Clay before, though. She'd known he was handsome and exciting. But she'd never considered how much he had to give to a family.

She suddenly realized she had been selfish all those years ago. She had been delighted when her father signed up to get a foster kid, and she had just assumed it would be a good arrangement for whoever came to the ranch.

But she hadn't thought about it once after Clay was here. She didn't remember ever asking if he was happy on the ranch.

It was too late to ask now, though, she told herself as she started up the steps to the house. Clay and Jeremy were clomping along behind her talking about why that pig in the barn was so small.

"I never knew about your suitcase," Allie turned to say as she reached the door. "I should have looked around in the bunkhouse to gather up your things. I could have sent everything to you. It was yours."

Clay shrugged as he swung the door open for her. "They wouldn't have let me keep my stuff anyway in prison. Against the rules."

"Then I could have put the suitcase someplace safer," she said as she stepped into the kitchen. "No one has lived in the bunkhouse for several years now. Someone could have walked off with it and we would never have known."

"The case is pretty shabby. I don't think anyone would want it," Clay said as he stood in the doorway.

"Still," Allie said.

"I could bring the sketches inside so you can look at them," Clay said as he continued standing in the doorway. "That would probably be more comfortable than looking at them in the bunkhouse. We didn't leave the heat on when we left this morning."

"We have plenty of propane for the heater," Allie said. "I don't want you and Randy freezing out there just to save a few pennies."

"We probably only have one cold snap left," Clay said. "Then everything will be warming up. I'll go get the sketches then while you get Jeremy set for his nap."

Allie nodded. He stepped back out of the house, and Allie stood there with her nephew. She wondered if Clay had liked living in the bunkhouse. She remembered some of the older ranch hands complaining about the cold nights out there, but she had not worried about it back then. The main house had been cold, too, in the winter. She was beginning to feel, though, as if her family had failed Clay in some way over the years.

Clay might not be as innocent as he said he had been on that night, but she had to admit that she and her family were not blameless, either. The truth was that she needed to consider that Clay might be telling the truth. Had she been wrong about her brother?

Clay was glad he was alone in the bunkhouse when he pulled that old suitcase out from under the bed. A thick layer of dust lay on top of the brown-checked hard shell. The whole thing wasn't much bigger than a duffel bag. He'd always thought it might have belonged to his mother because it had carried the faint smell of lavender, and he had believed a perfume bottle had been broken in it at some time. Thinking she liked lavender helped Clay form a picture of his mother. He always thought she'd been a pretty lady. He had no pictures of either of his parents, though.

A gold catch closed the case, and he pressed on its sides to make it snap open. The dust went flying as the suitcase vibrated sharply. He lifted the lid and peered inside. The stained gold lining was frayed in places. He had an old T-shirt laid out on top of everything. He took that out and set it on his bed. A brown bag of marbles nestled in a corner of the suitcase. He had collected a few cat's-eye marbles when he was seven or so. And there was a broken watch that had been a gift to him from a social worker once. That was the Christmas when he was between foster homes and had been in some kind of an institution. He'd been surprised and grateful for the timepiece. It was one of the few presents he'd gotten that hadn't come from a charity gift drive.

Ah, there it was, Clay thought as he found

the sturdy folder. He'd used those in high school. This one must be the sketches, he thought. He was half-afraid to open the thing up and look. He remembered each of the drawings he had made of Allie, but he wasn't sure if his mind had persuaded him over the years that they were better than they really were. He'd thought at the time that they were fine drawings, very fine. But he had not known much about art then. At least in prison he'd been able to borrow a few art books from the library.

Suddenly, Clay decided he'd take the folder into the house and open it with Allie. He wanted to be able to judge if she actually wanted the sketches even seen by anyone else. Once they sold the sketches, Clay wouldn't be able to control where they were shown.

Clay noticed the silence in the air as he walked toward the main house. He was so used to the constant low hum of noise in prison that he needed to remind himself that this quiet was normal. Nothing was wrong. The sun was shining, the sky was blue and the clouds were low in the east.

A quick knock at the door gained Clay an invitation to come inside.

Allie had changed back into her jeans and sweater while he'd been in the bunkhouse. She hadn't taken the makeup off her face, though, and he enjoyed seeing her more polished look. He liked seeing Allie dressed up for the day. She had tiny pearls earrings on, as well.

"We can sit over here," Allie said as she walked to the wall and flipped a switch so the hanging fixture over the table lit up. "My father is lying down with Jeremy to help him go to sleep, but he'll be out in a few minutes. Jeremy runs around with all this energy, but if we can convince him to lie down he nods off pretty quickly."

"We'll wait for your dad then," Clay said as he set the folder down. The table's surface was a polished oak that was worn. There was a burn scar to the right of the center. A pair of salt and pepper shakers stood in the middle of the table.

Allie pulled out a chair and he did, too.

"Before we even look at the sketches," Clay said as he settled himself on the hardback furniture, "I want to be sure that you know I'm okay if you'd rather not have anything done with them. The drawings are of you. You own them as much as I do."

Allie sat down and didn't even hesitate. "But if they can help you—"

Clay shook his head. "I'll get by. I can draw new sketches. This collector's thing might be a two-second wonder anyway. Nothing says it will last."

Allie leaned forward. "But that's all the more reason to use whatever sketches you have. If you wait to draw new ones, you might miss the opportunity."

Clay had never been able to resist the sincere look in Allie's green eyes. Her whole face beamed when she was doing something she believed in. She'd pulled her auburn hair back in a clip, but several strands hung free.

"If anyone pays for the sketches," Clay said, "the money will go to you."

"No," Allie gasped. Her eyes went dark, and she looked upset. "It's your work."

"It's your face," he countered.

"But I couldn't take it," she said, shaking her head. Even more hair fell from the clip, but she didn't push it back. She just kept staring at him. "You're already working here for free."

"Room and board," Clay said with a grin. "And I plan to eat a lot."

He meant to lighten the mood, but she just sat there shaking her head.

"The ranch needs the money," Clay finally coaxed her softly. "More than I do right now."

"I'll take care of the ranch," Allie protested. "I've been doing it for years. We get by."

"If you have the money, you could spend

more time here," he said softly. He wondered then if that's why he wanted her to have it. He had visions of days spent with her as they worked with those horses. They used to make a good team doing that.

Allie didn't answer for several moments, but when she did her voice sounded resolute. "No. It's your fresh start. It's only fair that anything that comes goes to you. You're a—"

Allie stopped and didn't continue.

"A foster kid?" Clay asked bitterly. "An ex-con?"

"I was going to say you're a good man," Allie said quietly. "But you're also too generous."

Clay was speechless. No one had ever accused him of being good before.

A soft footfall sounded in the hall, and Mr. Nelson stepped out of the shadows into the kitchen.

"He's finally sleeping," the older man whispered. "Had quite a time getting him to close his eyes."

Mr. Nelson drew up a chair and sat down, leaning his elbows on the table. He took a deep breath and then looked directly at Clay. "The boy asked me if an uncle can become a dad."

"What?" Clay sat back like he'd been shot.

"He likes having an uncle," Mr. Nelson said.

"Only one day and he's taken with it. But he must want a dad, too."

"But he's never said anything," Allie protested. "At least not that I've heard. Maybe he talks to Hannah about it, though."

They were all silent.

"I'm sure this is all very difficult for Hannah," the older man finally said. "She's never even mentioned to me that she's dating anyone. As far as I know, she's still mourning her life with Mark."

"But Mark's not dead," Clay protested.

"He was in a coma for years," Mr. Nelson said. "No wonder she doesn't say anything to Jeremy. You'd have to explain to him then that he couldn't even talk to his father."

"He's a bright boy," Allie said. "It's not surprising that he's starting to question things."

They were all quiet and Clay sat there, still stunned that he was a little boy's uncle, if not by blood then by choice. He didn't like to picture the hard bumps Jeremy would encounter in the coming years. Even if he ever did learn that Mark was his father, what would that mean? Clay wasn't sure if Mark would ever be able to fill that father's role for Jeremy. And Clay might be around the ranch for only the year he was assigned. If he wasn't there to watch Jeremy grow up, either, then he wanted the boy to know he had someone in his corner.

"The money can go to Jeremy," Clay said, catching Allie's eye. "If you don't want it, we can set up a college fund for the boy." Allie didn't say anything for a minute, so he continued. "I want him to know he has a family who will look out for him."

"You'd do that?" Allie asked. She blinked them back, but Clay could see she had tears in her eyes.

He didn't trust himself to speak, so he nodded.

They sat there in silence until Mr. Nelson stood up. "I'm going to put some coffee on. Anyone else want some?"

Allie and Clay both nodded.

"We should look at the sketches before getting our coffee, though," Allie said. "We don't want to spill on them."

Clay opened the folder.

"Ah." Allie sighed when Clay lifted out the first sketch.

He smiled. It was the drawing of Allie looking out her bedroom window. Black ink strokes outlined everything. She was looking up at the night sky, her face filled with longing.

"I called that one *Wishing on a Star*," Clay noted.

"It's perfect," Allie said. "That shows exactly how I felt. I was so full of longing to experience life. To go places and see things. I thought I would burst."

Clay held up another sketch.

"Here's one of you cooking in the kitchen," Clay said.

He remembered seeing her that day. She was so intent on cracking the eggs that she was biting down on her bottom lip slightly. Her hair had more red in it back then, and the morning light made her curls shine.

"You have me in my mother's apron," Allie said.

Clay nodded and took another sketch out of the folder.

"And my horse," Allie exclaimed. She had almost the same expression on her face now as she'd had back then. "I loved my Peony. She died not long after you left."

Clay stopped midreach. "I'm sorry."

Allie nodded. "It was a hard time for me. I felt like I'd lost my best friend."

Clay didn't dare ask if it was the horse or him that she had missed so much. He did notice that she put her finger on the sketch and traced the horse, though.

"Maybe we should keep that one back," Clay suggested. "You might want to have it."

Allie looked up and smiled. "I would. Thanks."

Clay nodded. Whenever Allie smiled, her whole face lit up. He'd always thought that was one reason he sketched her. She was so alive. Now, seeing her pleasure in the sketches, though, he wondered if he hadn't made them for this very moment. When Allie smiled at him like that, everything was right in his world.

He wondered suddenly why there was no give in him when it came to his insistence that Allie believe what he said about the robbery. He knew he was innocent. Would it be enough if he just started now and worked forward, ignoring what she thought he had done on that night so long ago? He wasn't sure.

"Ready for coffee?" Mr. Nelson asked from where he stood by the counter. "We'll want to look at the sketches later, too. Maybe Mark would enjoy seeing them. Did you ever show any of them to him?"

"No." Clay started gathering up the drawings. "I'm not sure how he'd like them. So much time has passed and, well, wouldn't Mark notice that Allie looks different today than she did back then?"

Clay looked over at Allie for an answer.

"He's never said anything to me about that,"

she said. "Maybe he can't remember what I used to look like. I've seen him about once a month all this time. The doctors have always told us that we shouldn't mention how much time has passed to Mark. But I wonder if he knows."

Clay thought Allie looked worried.

"I'm sure everything will be fine," Clay said.

"It has to be," Allie added.

Clay nodded. He would just as soon stay back at the ranch tomorrow and work with the horses. He knew that wasn't going to happen, though. He had to go visit with Mark. But what if seeing him brought that robbery back to Mark's mind?

Chapter Twelve

Allie dressed with care the following morning. The sky was overcast, and very little light came inside her bedroom even though it was seven o'clock already. She felt self-conscious after the conversation yesterday suggesting Mark might wonder why she looked different from how she had at sixteen. She had deliberately kept her hair styled the same for the past half-dozen years because she thought Mark would find it familiar in his coma. She meant it to be comforting, not to deceive him about the passage of time.

She took the stairs down to the kitchen, intending to make some eggs and toast to go with the coffee. She glanced out the window and saw that Randy's brown pickup had been moved from where it was yesterday. She thought she'd heard him drive in last night.

He'd be ready for work this morning. The lights were on in the bunkhouse, so she assumed Clay and Randy were getting ready for the day.

While the eggs finished cooking, Allie changed the page on the calendar hanging on the wall. She remembered she'd had to do the same thing the last time she'd been back at the ranch. Her father just let the days flow over him.

Jeremy and her father came into the kitchen, and she dished up breakfast for them.

"We're going to start working on the hay wagon today," her father said as he settled himself and Jeremy on their chairs. The table was already set with dishes and silverware. "I've talked to Clay. He has some ideas. We'll make sure the wagon's ready for Sunday."

"You're still set on doing this Easter processional?" Allie asked as she set the platters in the center of the table.

Her father nodded as he held out his hands to Jeremy and to Allie. "Now that Clay is here we should have no problem."

Allie didn't answer.

"Well?" her father said.

"I'll stop at the hardware store in Dry Creek on our way to the nursing home," Allie said as she took her father's hand. "We'll all need new hats this year."

One of the traditions with the processional was for those riding on the wagon to all wear new white Stetsons. Mark would enjoy having his hat early.

Allie bowed her head as her father started to pray aloud. She let his words of gratefulness speak for her. Her family had endured its share of hard times, but her parents had both believed in being thankful for what God had provided.

They finished eating and she had the table cleared when she heard footsteps on the porch.

She opened the door after the knock and saw Clay standing there. He wore the sheepskin coat and his black Stetson. The temperature outside was low enough that a cloud of white air showed when he spoke.

"Ready to go?" Clay was hunched slightly like he was cold.

"We can take my dad's SUV," she said as she stepped out of the door, her purse slung over her shoulder. "I suppose you want to drive?"

The freezing air hit her when she moved past the doorway.

He grinned. "You know I do. But I'd rather take that old pickup if you don't mind. Your dad should have his vehicle in case he needs to go someplace."

Allie nodded as she closed the door behind her. "You're right. My little car isn't much good on country roads in the winter, so he wouldn't want to drive that for any distance."

She remembered how much Clay enjoyed driving that old pickup around. A person would have thought it was a sports car rather than a worn-down ranching vehicle. Clay had volunteered to haul bales out to the horses for the night feeding many times just so he could get behind the wheel. Her father had already mentioned that he'd hired one of the Elkton wranglers to drive the pickup over to the prison in Deer Lodge and leave it there for when Clay was released.

Clay backed up so she could climb into the pickup without having to cross the puddle that had formed beside the cab. Allie's teeth shivered as they drove off the ranch and headed down the gravel road into Dry Creek.

"I can't wait to see Mark," Clay said after a few miles.

Allie nodded. "He will look different. Just so you're prepared. He's thinner now. He lost most of his muscles. They have him doing rehab work, but he still looks like a starving man."

"I wouldn't expect him to win a beauty contest," Clay said. "Is he strong, though? Should I shake his hand? Hug him? Or do I keep my distance? I can do whatever is best for him."

Allie relaxed. Clay was asking the right kind of questions. He knew her brother would need special care. "I'm sure he'd appreciate a handshake."

They spent the rest of the ride into Dry Creek reminiscing about their days on the ranch with Mark. Allie had forgotten half of the things that Clay remembered. They made her smile. Those had been good times.

"I thought we'd stop at the hardware store," Allie said when they were at the outskirts of the small town. "We always get—"

"White hats!" Clay finished for her in excitement. "I remember Mark talking about that. He called them the Nelson Easter bonnets."

"My mom and I got them, too," Allie said with a grin. "That's why he used to joke about them. Sometimes Mom would put a flower in the band around her Stetson. We used to wear these pretty Easter dresses, but she said we needed to have a rancher's hat to show where we came from."

Allie wished it was that easy now to be sure of where she belonged and what direction her life should take. Ever since Clay had come back, things had seemed unsettled.

Clay opened the door to the hardware store for Allie and stood to the side while she entered. He could hear the deep-toned chorus of welcome from what he figured was the group of men sitting around that potbelly stove in the middle of the store. Clay had never sat with the men there; Mr. Nelson had invited him once when they were in town, but Clay had preferred to slip over to the café with Allie and get a soda.

When Allie had stepped into the store, he followed her, closing the door behind him. A large store window looked out to the street. A cashier's counter was on the left, and he saw that the pastor, Matthew Curtis, stood there tallying up something in a ledger. Rows of shelves held the merchandise.

"Good to have you stop by, Clay," the pastor said with a smile.

Time had passed. Since Clay had been sent to prison, the man's dark hair had gained a few gray streaks. Laugh lines showed by his eyes. But his welcome was as warm as ever.

"Thanks," Clay said. He remembered Allie telling him once that the pastor worked part-time in the hardware store so he could put money aside for the college funds for his twin boys. The boys had to be past that stage now, though. Or, close to it.

"We came for hats," Clay finally said as he glanced over to where Allie was chatting with a half-dozen old, grizzled ranchers. They were sitting in an assortment of hard-backed chairs that were ringed around that potbellied stove. He could tell by the looks on their faces that they adored Allie. She was no doubt talking crops and horses with them like she'd done since she was a kid.

"Easter hats?" the pastor asked as he walked over to a shelf on the back wall.

"Yes," Clay said as he stood still.

He thought he was doing fine until Allie looked back at him and frowned slightly. "Come on over and say hi to everyone."

He could spot a phony smile a hundred feet away, and he was much closer than that to those old ranchers. If they tried to smile any harder, he was afraid they'd strain something.

The only sound in the place as Clay walked over was the creak in the ladder as the pastor climbed up to bring down the hats.

Finally, one of the ranchers slowly rose to his feet. "The wife tells me you're reformed now. Some kind of an artist."

The man didn't sound impressed, and he didn't offer to shake hands.

"I draw a bit," Clay admitted. He didn't hold out his hand, either.

"Learn that in the joint?" another man asked. He didn't show any inclination to stand.

The rest of the men sat there looking at him suspiciously. The smiles were gone. Clay was relieved for that at least.

"I expect you learned more than how to draw when you were in prison," the man continued. "Or maybe you taught the boys there something, what with your history and all."

"What do you mean by that?" Clay asked.

The other man didn't answer, but Clay noted that Allie's face had reddened. She was embarrassed. He supposed he shouldn't blame her. No one liked to hang out with a foster kid turned ex-con.

He could hear the pastor climbing back down the ladder.

"I got an assortment of sizes to try on," he said cheerfully.

Clay turned and saw the pastor carrying an armload of white Stetson hats over to the counter. He looked like he hadn't heard the accusation hanging in the air.

"Thank you," Allie said with relief in her voice as she gestured for Clay to meet her over at the counter. "We'll be quick about it. We need the smallest one you have for my nephew. Then we'll take three in a size seven and—" She looked at Clay. "Do you know the size you need? There's a tag inside the hat you have on that probably says."

"It's seven and five-eighths." Clay didn't need to remove his hat. When a man didn't own much, he usually knew what he had.

The pastor pulled a hat off the top of the stack and put it with the others he'd already set aside. Then he put them all in a beige plastic bag with a sales slip.

Clay felt self-conscious because he knew the ranchers were listening to everything he and Allie said. But none of the men voiced any opinions. He supposed they thought even troublemakers were entitled to wear a new hat.

Clay followed Allie's lead and they were soon out of the hardware store with five brand-new Stetson hats in their possession. The bright white felt in the hats was accented with bands of brass-tipped leather cords.

"They look great," Clay said when they climbed back into the pickup. He set the bag with the hats on the seat between them. "I've never had such a good-looking Stetson."

He hated to see Allie subdued like this when she'd been looking forward to something as simple as a new Easter bonnet. "You'll look great in your new hat, too."

She smiled at him, but it was a halfhearted gesture.

The drive to the nursing home outside Miles City was quiet. The land was flat, and they didn't see many vehicles on the freeway. The sky had darkened, and Clay suspected it would snow before the day was over.

"They don't mean to be unfair," Allie said at one point. "Back at the hardware store."

"It's okay," Clay assured her. He shouldn't be disappointed. A few people in Dry Creek had been happy to see him. That would have to be enough. "Some people don't understand."

"They're good men usually," she added.

"I know," Clay said, and he meant it. Those men would do almost anything for a neighbor in trouble. But he was an outsider to them, and he always had been. They probably didn't like seeing him with Allie either, and he didn't blame them. No woman needed to be tagged as a friend to an ex-con.

Of course, saying anything like that to Allie would only get her hackles up. So, he asked Allie about her life in Jackson Hole, and they talked a little of happier things.

Clay had driven through Miles City before he saw the sign for the nursing home. He turned off the freeway and slowed down to enter the lane leading to the long frame building. Clay could tell from the soft gray paint and white trim that someone had tried to make the structure look inviting. There was a large yard at the front of the home, but the grass was dead and patches of snow were scattered around.

"All of the rooms have windows at least," Allie said as Clay parked the pickup. "Mark is on the west side, so he sees the sun go down every day."

Clay tried to look positively at everything. He knew from prison how important seeing the sun was, but he also knew that having a view was seldom enough to make up for being confined for whatever reason. He wondered if Mark felt trapped in this place. Or was he so sick that he didn't care?

Allie brought in one of the size seven Stetsons for Mark. They left the rest of the hats in that bag in the pickup.

Clay stopped when they came to the steps going into the building. He turned to Allie. "Do I look okay?"

She must have known what he was asking because she studied him. "Smile when you see him. You look younger when you do that.

And keep your hat on if you can. That hides your eyes a little."

He grinned. "What's wrong with my eyes?"

"They've seen a lot of life," Allie replied. "It shows."

"I'd seen a lot of things before I met Mark, too." Clay turned and opened the main door to the place. "My eyes have always looked like this."

Clay noticed it was not silent as they walked down the corridors. People were talking in hushed tones, but it all added up to a medium hum that didn't stop.

"Here it is," Allie said when they came to one of the small rooms. She looked up at Clay. "I'll go in first and let him know you're with me."

"That's probably best." Clay tried to rein in his excitement. He knew Mark wouldn't be able to handle an exuberant greeting from him so, regardless of the joy he felt inside, he took a deep breath and told himself to calm down.

Clay heard the surprised cry inside the room as Mark realized Allie was there.

After a couple of minutes, Allie came back to the door. She had a huge grin on her face and tears falling down her cheeks. "Come in."

Clay stepped inside and saw his old friend. "Mark."

Despite the warnings he'd had, Clay was shocked. His friend was gaunt. He looked worse than men who'd been in solitary confinement for a month. Mark had grown a few inches taller since Clay had seen him last, but he probably weighed forty pounds less. His skin was slightly yellow. His black hair was poorly cut, and he'd nicked himself shaving. He wore blue-and-white-striped pajamas. His brown eyes were shining, though, as he looked at Clay.

"It's about time," Mark said as he took a feeble step toward Clay. "I'm not contagious, you know. People don't need to worry about seeing me. I just had a—" Mark got a confused look on his face as he hesitated "—an accident, I guess."

"You've had a hard time," Clay agreed softly as he walked farther into the room.

Mark stared at Clay for a few seconds. "I need to lie back down."

Clay nodded.

"Come sit and talk to me, though," Mark said as he lay down on the hospital bed. "I want you to tell me how everyone is." He paused and then grinned. "Especially Hannah. I guess she's still mad at me."

Clay took his time walking over to the one

chair beside the bed. He didn't know what to say.

It was silent for a moment and then Mark turned to Allie, who stood by the door. "Can you get us some sodas from the machine at the end of the hall?"

She looked at Clay before nodding and leaving.

"You can tell me about it now," Mark said after Allie was gone. "Hannah hasn't come by. I tried to call her number, and the phone was disconnected. I know Sammy Yates would like to ask her out, so I don't want him making moves on her while I am laid up in here. I want to take her to the prom, and I haven't had a chance to even ask her."

Clay swallowed. "There's no hurry. You've got time."

"You haven't seen them together?" Mark asked anxiously.

"No." Clay was glad he could answer that at least.

Mark seemed worn out from the conversation and lay on his bed for some time just looking over at Clay.

"Have you been working out?" Mark finally asked, studying Clay.

"Just hanging out," Clay said as he tried

to look a little less bulky in the heavy coat he wore.

Mark kept eyeing him, though.

"You're different," he said quietly. "You look—" Mark seemed to search for the word "—settled."

Clay sat up at that. "What do you mean?"

"Have you finished reading the Gospel of Luke?" Mark asked. "I've been wanting to talk to you about it. I keep going over it again and again. It was a good challenge from the church. I think it's true, you know."

"I read it yesterday." Clay had lain on the mattress on the kitchen floor in the bunkhouse last night and couldn't sleep, so he pulled the Bible off the low shelf. The account of Jesus had drawn him in, and he hadn't been able to stop reading until he finished.

"I'm glad we're doing the Easter processional," Mark said. His voice was getting weaker, and he had to pause between the words. "You're still in on that, aren't you?"

"Yes, I'm in," Clay said.

"It's important to me to be there," Mark said, slower yet. Each word seemed an effort now. "I never understood about Easter until now."

Clay saw the truth on his friend's face. Mark

knew something about the Easter story that he didn't. "I'll see that you get there."

Allie came back then with three cans of cola.

"I need to take a nap now," Mark whispered. "But I'll see you early on Sunday. Real early. We have to be there for the Resurrection."

Clay nodded, and Allie quietly set one of the cans of soda on Mark's nightstand. He'd already closed his eyes.

"See that Hannah doesn't go out with anyone else," Mark whispered as Clay walked to the door.

Clay turned around, and Mark had opened his eyes again.

"You just rest now," Clay said softly. "Don't worry about a thing."

Clay left the room with Allie.

They were silent as they walked through the corridors and exited the building. Snow began to fall as Clay started to drive back to Dry Creek.

"Are you okay?" he asked Allie after a few miles. She'd been quiet.

She nodded. "He's come so far, but he has a long way still to go. I just feel bad for him."

"Is there a reason the doctors don't tell him how long he's been out of it?" Clay asked.

"They say it's better for him if he figures it

out for himself," Allie said. "They keep him away from mirrors and calendars. They say that when he's ready to absorb the information, his mind will let him know it."

They drove awhile in companionable silence.

"Do you know about Hannah?" Clay finally asked. "Does she still have any feelings for Mark?"

"I don't know. She never says. She did go to see Mark a lot when he was first in the coma, but after Jeremy was born she didn't go as often. Of course, it was probably hard with the baby. Then I think she gave up. All I know is that she finished a nursing program and has signed up for some kind of specialized training. She's taking the course now back east. That's why Jeremy is here with us for a couple of weeks."

"She's not engaged, though?" Clay persisted.

Allie hesitated. "She hasn't said anything. Jeremy has talked about a man his mother knows, though—Sammy something. Jeremy doesn't seem to like the man, but I don't know what Hannah has planned."

"Not Sammy Yates?" Clay protested in alarm.

Allie frowned. "I think so. I didn't know

much about him, but he was in school with Mark and Hannah."

"Well, that's not good," Clay said.

"What's wrong with Sammy?"

"He's stealing Mark's girl."

"But—" Allie started and then stopped. "Does it matter now?"

There seemed to be no answer for that, and they continued the drive in thoughtful silence. Clay noticed the wind starting to blow as they got near Dry Creek.

"We should stop at the café and get something to go," Allie said as they came to the first building in the small town. The sky had darkened by now, and it was clear a storm was coming. "It's past noon and they will have already eaten at the ranch. Not that they won't all have room for a hamburger, too. We'll want to be able to get right to work and make sure everything is closed up tight in the barn before this storm hits."

The strip of asphalt running through the small town widened a bit in front of the café. Cement steps led up to the door, and red-and-white-checked curtains fluttered over the glass-paned windows on each side of the entry. Three other mud-spattered pickups were parked next to the café, and Clay slipped his vehicle into place at the end of the line.

When he stepped out of the pickup, Clay was grateful for the sheepskin coat that he still wore. He opened one of the front flaps and wrapped that around a shivering Allie as they hurried over to the stairs. The rush of the wind made them laugh as they pushed against it all the way. Finally, Clay opened the door and they tumbled into the café, breathless and still laughing.

"It's getting fierce out there," a pleasant-looking waitress with red hair said as she paused in her path across the café, a full coffeepot in her hand. "Have a seat anywhere and I'll get to you after I refill the cups over there."

She inclined her head to where four of the ranchers sat. Clay recognized them from this morning at the hardware store. He nodded in their direction, but none of them nodded back.

Clay decided to ignore them. Life was too short to butt heads against everyone who had an inclination to suspect other people of everything they might have done in life.

Clay followed Allie to one of the side tables. Before he sat down, he took his coat off and laid it over one of the empty chairs at their table. He liked the cozy warmth inside the café.

The woman came back quickly with an

order pad in one hand and a pencil in the other. "Sorry about that."

"Not a problem, Lois," Allie said.

So this was Lois, Clay thought in delight. Her hair was too bright to be natural, but her smile looked 100 percent genuine. She had pretty amber eyes and well-defined cheekbones. He'd guess she was about forty years old, so she'd be a few years younger than Randy. He looked at her hands and didn't see any kind of a ring. Her white apron was neat, and it covered a blue T-shirt and basic jeans.

He'd known Allie was giving the order while he studied Lois, but he was suddenly aware of an ominous silence and looked over at Allie.

She was not happy with him. Her lips were pursed and only relaxed slightly when she spoke. "I've been asking how you want your hamburger."

"Well-done with grilled onions if you have them," he said, looking up at Lois.

"Not a problem," the waitress confirmed as she added a note to her order pad. "Now for the pie. We have apple, cherry and a lime chiffon that I made. I make a different chiffon pie every day. The apple and cherry are excellent, too. We have them delivered from a bakery in Miles City."

"We'll get five pieces of pie then," Allie said. "I'll take apple for my dad and nephew. A cherry for me. Clay, what do you want?"

Her eyes glowered at him, but he answered politely. "I'd love a slice of cherry, too."

"And Randy?" Allie asked.

"Randy Collins?" Lois echoed the question. Clay was gratified to see her face brightened up even more than what looked like her usual good cheer. "He always gets a slice of chiffon. Lemon, raspberry. Like I said it's lime today, and I know he'd order that if he were here."

Clay grinned. The Randy he used to know would rather eat sawdust than something as girlie as chiffon pie. In fact, Clay distinctly remembered Randy chastising him for eating cherry pie. That's when the other man had explained that a wrangler ate only apple pie unless it was Thanksgiving. On that day it was permissible to have a slice of pumpkin, as well.

Clay chuckled, and both women looked at him askance.

"Everyone will love a piece of pie," he said. The words were meaningless, but at least no one looked at him funny any longer. "In fact, give me an extra slice of apple."

Fifteen minutes later, Clay and Allie were leaving the café, carrying white bags of take-out. The wind was whipping around even stronger, so Clay walked close enough to shelter Allie from some of the worst of it.

He opened the door for Allie, and she climbed into the pickup. He handed her all of the food, and she set it on the floor at her feet. Then Clay shut the door and fought his way around to the driver's side.

He was freezing by the time he opened his door and got inside.

"I hope this blizzard goes away before Sunday," Clay said as he blew on his hands for a few seconds to warm them before he put them on the cold steering wheel. "Mark couldn't be out in a storm like this one."

"It won't last that many days," Allie said. "According to the weather forecast it'll be gone by Wednesday."

"Good." Clay's meeting with his new art agent had been set for seven o'clock Wednesday morning at this café.

Clay turned the key and started the pickup. Then he backed out and got started on the road to the Nelson ranch. The smell of the hamburgers had him pressing a little harder on the gas pedal.

They had gone a few miles when Allie looked over at him. He was just beginning to wonder why she was so quiet when she spoke.

"I saw you checking out Lois," Allie announced haughtily. "She just moved here a few months ago. She's pretty, don't you think?"

Clay smiled. Allie was trying to pretend she didn't care, but she did look put out about it, which gave him more hope than it probably should have.

"Just doing a favor for someone," Clay replied mildly.

Allie snorted. "Don't expect me to believe that. You don't even know anyone around here in need of a favor except me and Mark and Dad and—" She stopped and her eyes got wide. "Randy?"

Clay nodded with a grin.

Allie hooted in laughter. "I wondered what was up when she said Randy was ordering all that chiffon pie. He's more a meat-and-potatoes kind of guy. And I don't think he even likes lime."

"I'm sure he doesn't," Clay agreed. "That's why I asked for the extra slice of apple pie. He'd be feeling pretty low if everyone else was having apple and cherry and he was stuck looking at his piece of lime chiffon."

Allie nodded, her eyes still dancing with merriment.

Clay saw her smile periodically as they finished the trip to the ranch. He was glad to know she was still a romantic at heart. She was probably picturing Randy and Lois getting together at some point. It took a real man to eat chiffon pie to prove his love, Clay told himself.

He sat there a moment before the realization struck him like a bolt out of the sky that he wasn't sure he'd be willing to eat chiffon pie. Was he too set in his ways for love? Was he asking too much of Allie to insist she believe that he was telling the truth about his innocence in that robbery four years ago? Would it be enough if he put the past behind them and just moved on from here? Or would her unwillingness to believe him on that one point always be with them? Agreeing on chiffon pie wasn't the same as agreeing on a matter of truth.

Maybe he didn't have what it took for love. Maybe he was like those daffodils that were starting to bloom around the church. They would be dying without that tarp. Unfortunately, there were no plastic wraps for people's emotions.

He was surprised to realize he would be disappointed if the sunrise service didn't happen. He planned to read the Gospel of Luke again tonight. He wasn't sure he understood everything. And what he did understand seemed impossible to him.

He thought of Mark and their old pledge

to study up on the Gospel of Luke. He'd read it through several times already, but he'd go slower with it tonight and see if he could find any clues on how to know what were the right things to say to Mark.

Chapter Thirteen

"We need some work on that wagon," Randy said as Clay stepped inside the barn. Allie had gone into the main house with the take-out bags, but Clay knew he would enjoy his food more if he checked on the progress out here first.

Clay walked over to where Randy was standing by the Easter wagon. Rickety gray planks leaned inward as they formed the two sides of the wagon. The back was open. The bed was made of the same kind of wood, but seemed to be in better shape. Long gaps showed where the wood had splintered away, and rusty nails held the whole thing together.

"There's some plywood up in the hayloft," Clay said. "Maybe we could use that to shore up this thing."

The wind was blowing flakes of snow into

the barn through the opening that led out to the attached corral. There was a sliding door that could be closed, but no one had done it yet. The horses were bunched together near the barn wall, but so far they hadn't come back into the barn. Clay didn't blame them for preferring to stay outside as long as possible.

"I hope the blizzard is gone by the time we have to drive this wagon into Dry Creek," Randy said as he squatted down to point out some boards low on one side. "It could fall apart from the rattling."

"We'll get at it in a bit," Clay said. "But Allie brought everyone hamburgers and pie at the café in Dry Creek, and we'll want to eat that while it's warm."

"Sounds really good," Randy said as he straightened. "Mr. Nelson made up some soup and sandwiches earlier, but I'm hungry already."

"I figured as much," Clay said.

The two of them went into the house and washed up. Allie already had on the table the hamburgers in their wrappers and the pieces of pie in the plastic containers the café had given them. Mr. Nelson and Jeremy were finishing playing a game of some kind and were at the table shortly after Clay and Randy got there.

"I hear you like chiffon pie," Clay said innocently as he and Randy sat at the table.

Allie grinned as she sat down to join them. "Lime," she added.

Randy nodded grimly. "How many pieces of that were left?"

"You wanted more?" Clay asked in astonishment. Maybe he had misjudged the wrangler. "Of chiffon?"

Randy shook his head and leaned forward with his elbows on the table. "I just want to know how many pieces of her pie are left. There are a couple of the guys at the Elkton Ranch that go in and buy a piece of her chiffon pie every day. They even bought some of her kiwi chiffon! They've started getting it to go so I know they don't eat it, but they have no business making time with Lois that way. They stand and flirt with her while she dishes up the pie."

Clay couldn't help but grin. "I didn't see any ring on her finger. I guess they figure she's not spoken for yet."

"I'm working on it," Randy said testily, glowering at him. "I figure she'd want to know me some before she'll agree to go out with me."

"That's a good plan," Allie said soothingly. "Be friends first."

Clay didn't comment. That wasn't how a man went about all of this—not if he had competition for the lady of his heart.

"But those Elkton guys are crowding me," Randy said. "I want a spectacular first date, and I'm not ready for it yet."

"Maybe they just like pie," Clay offered.

"It's chiffon," Randy protested. "Nothing but air and some frilly stuff. Those guys don't like it. It's a woman's pie."

By that time, Allie had the hamburgers passed around. Mr. Nelson said the blessing and everyone started to eat. It was silent until Allie started to give out the slices of pie.

"That green one must be mine," Randy said, his voice sounding dejected while his eyes watched the slice of apple pie that was making its way over to Mr. Nelson. Randy didn't say anything, but a deep sigh rose from his chest.

"Don't worry," Allie said to Randy. "Clay has you covered on this one."

Then she handed him the piece of apple pie. "He insisted we get this extra for you."

Randy's face brightened immediately, and he looked over at Clay. "I owe you for this one, buddy."

Clay nodded but didn't say anything.

"Seriously," Randy continued. "I could have been nicer to you when you got here, and for you to do this—I'm insisting I pay you back some way."

"That's not necessary," Clay said.

Clay looked out the closest window. He wondered if Randy was suggesting they become friends. He didn't know what to say about that so he concentrated on the view from the window instead. Snow was falling in earnest now, large wet flakes coming down. "We better get going if we want to get those animals taken care of."

Allie was the first one out to the barn, and she reveled in the silence when she stepped inside the small door that was across from the house. The horses had made their way inside and were waiting by the feed trough. She'd stored the cortisone drops for their eyes in the tack room, so she figured she'd get those dispensed before she worried about getting another hay bale down from the loft.

She realized she was mighty cheerful considering a storm was coming their way. She had to admit she liked having chores to do again. Halfway through the barn, she heard a squeal and a series of rapid footsteps.

"Julie," she said as she squatted down to meet the miniature pig that was barreling toward her. When the animal got to her, its squeals intensified.

"Sorry," Allie said. "I didn't bring a treat for you."

She patted the pig on the head like she would a dog. It didn't seem to satisfy the animal much, though, because it kept making a racket.

The stallion suddenly neighed and stomped its foot. The pig looked up and stopped making noise at that signal. Allie smiled. It seemed the animals had things figured out among themselves.

The air blowing into the barn from the opening to the corral was getting colder, and Allie could see that the horses were wet. She walked to the tack room and brought back some of the old towels she kept out here for the very purpose of rubbing animals down when that happened. By the time she'd finished with the rubdowns, Clay was there to bring the hay down from the loft.

"Give them enough hay to get them to morning," Allie said as Clay was climbing the ladder. "That way we don't have to come out later."

"I'll do that," Clay said. "But I want to work on this wagon some this afternoon. I need to sort through the leather harnesses, too."

Allie nodded. She was grateful Clay was putting all he had into this Easter processional. She knew he was doing it for Mark, but she hoped it would also ease some of the tension between Clay and the older ranchers around here. She'd been upset when she'd seen how unfriendly they had been to Clay. Every man had a right to a second chance.

After Clay threw a couple of hay bales from the loft to the feed trough, he climbed down the ladder with a small bag of oats over his shoulder for the goat.

"You're going to have to earn this," Clay said to the brown-haired goat. Then he put some out for it.

Allie smiled. Her father used to say a man could tell which wranglers would make good ranchers by whether or not they talked to the animals in their care.

"Don't spend so much time out here that you forget about getting your sketches ready for that agent of yours," Allie cautioned. Clay might enjoy the animals, but it sounded like his future was brighter with his artwork.

"I've got time for it all," Clay said as Randy came inside the barn to join them.

Allie nodded. She hoped Clay was right. It would likely snow all day tomorrow, but the next day Clay would meet with his art agent.

She kept wanting to take another look at the collection of sketches he had done of her. She still couldn't believe what she saw. It was like he'd seen her emotions in all her everyday tasks. It might be strange to think of others looking at those drawings and seeing her emotions, but it also made her feel good, like she would be connected with all of those people in some way.

She wondered suddenly what would happen if the agent didn't like the way she looked.

"Are you doing some new sketches?" Allie asked Clay. "Maybe you should. For your meeting."

She'd feel better if the agent has something to choose from.

Clay nodded. "Last night I did some sketches of the stallion and the goat. I want to get a few more of the horses tomorrow."

"Good," Allie said. She didn't want Clay's success as an artist to rest on drawings of her. He would be safer to focus on the horses. Everyone loved pictures of animals.

Chapter Fourteen

Early Wednesday morning, Clay woke up and saw a layer of snow on the sills of the bunkhouse windows. He relied on the yard light to show the white flakes since the sun had not risen yet. Clay looked at the illuminated hands on the alarm clock he'd left by his mattress and saw that it was a little after five o'clock.

He didn't need to get up for an hour, he told himself as he pulled the covers tighter around his shoulders. He was comfortable as long as he stayed where he was. The floor under his mattress was freezing, and he had no desire to put his feet on it. He smiled as he remembered that Randy had vowed last night that he was getting up before Clay this morning to build a blaze in the fireplace. It was his way of paying Clay back for that piece of pie.

In Clay's opinion, no heat felt as homey as that coming from a nice fire.

"Randy," Clay called out.

"I'm getting up," the wrangler answered back with a yawn in his voice.

Clay must have slid back into sleep because the next thing he knew the air in the bunkhouse was tolerable and the red rooster was crowing. Clay could hear someone moving around in the other room, so he looked at the alarm clock and saw it was six o'clock. He had an hour to get himself into Dry Creek for the meeting with the art agent.

Clay dressed with care, and before it was time for him to leave, there was a knock on the bunkhouse door. Allie had come over with some hot sausage biscuits wrapped in tinfoil.

"You can come to the house to get yours," Allie said to Randy before holding out the biscuits to Clay. "But it's a long drive to Dry Creek, and I want you to know I'm praying for you and your meeting."

Randy nodded. "Break a leg."

"I think that's for actors," Clay said as he looked at them both. He wasn't used to support like this.

"You might see me in Dry Creek," Randy said. "I need to go in and check on those daffodils. I'll feed the animals here first, but I won't get in your way with your meeting."

Randy made the motion for zipping his lips. "I won't interrupt at all."

"I don't think we need to be that quiet." Clay hated to pull himself away from this cozy scene, but he wanted to leave plenty of time to get to the café before that art agent. The café opened at seven o'clock, so he needed to leave soon.

"I might need to go to Dry Creek, too," Allie said then. She looked a little shy. "I won't say anything, either."

"You can say anything you want," Clay assured her.

"Can I get a ride with you?" Allie asked Randy.

The man nodded, and the arrangements were all made.

The red pickup was cold when Clay climbed inside, but he set the hat bag on the floor of the passenger side. His was the only hat inside that bag, and he would have been tempted to pull it out and wear it for his meeting. But while it would look great for Easter morning, it seemed too dressed up for a Wednesday. Clay didn't want to look like he was putting on airs.

He drove in darkness, but the sun was beginning to rise when he pulled into Dry Creek.

He saw the lights go on in the café and noticed three other pickups were already gathered around the place. One of the vehicles was from the Redfern ranch, and it looked like someone was sitting in it, no doubt keeping warm until he could order a cup of coffee.

The light that went on must have been the signal that the café was ready for business because the door to the hardware store opened and five stocky ranchers came out and walked across the street. Clay waited a minute to follow them into the café.

Black-and-white squares covered the floor. Red stools stood at the counter. A pie stand on the counter held a fluffy pink pie. Clay liked this place, he thought as he settled himself at a table. Before he knew it, Lois brought around the coffeepot and poured him a cup.

"Can I get you something more?" she asked. The smell of bacon came from the back of the café, and he saw that those old ranchers had their menus in hand. "We've got buttermilk pancakes. Eggs any way you like them."

"Maybe later," Clay said and then asked, "What kind of chiffon pie do you have today?"

She beamed. "We don't serve pie until lunch, but it will be strawberry chiffon. I put it out early just because it's so pretty."

"I might get a piece to go later," Clay said. "My buddy Randy sure does like your pies."

She positively glowed at that.

"Some of the recipes are mine," Lois confided, her voice low. "I'm thinking of entering them in a dessert contest. The prize is a trip to Seattle to see the Space Needle. For two."

"For two," Clay repeated, trying to sound casual. "Who is the fortunate person who gets to go with you if you win?"

"Probably my mother," she said. "But it's too soon to know if I have a chance of winning."

"There's always a chance," Clay said. Even for Randy, he added silently to himself.

Clay looked over and noticed that the five ranchers were sending unfriendly looks his way. He figured they didn't want him holding up the waitress. Lois must have thought the same because she walked over and refilled their coffee cups while she noted what they wanted to eat.

It wasn't much longer before Clay's agent walked into the café, full of apologies for setting the meeting so early on a cold morning.

"You can't control the weather," Clay assured the man with a smile. "And I'm always up by now. A rancher does his best work in the early part of the day."

"I'm glad," the agent said. "I have to catch a plane later."

Clay forgot about everyone else as he opened his folder and started to show his agent the sketches of Allie. The man examined each drawing intently with a series of appreciative murmurs.

"These are excellent," the agent said at the end. "Just what you need."

"I have a few others." Clay pulled out the three drawings he had made of the horses and the goat.

The agent gave a warm chuckle when he looked at those. "Can you draw more of these?"

Clay nodded. He was on the verge of asking the agent a question when he heard the café door open with a bang. Angry footsteps sounded. Clay looked up and saw Randy standing in the open doorway with Allie trying to make her way around him.

"Where is that kid?" Randy bellowed, his voice rattling the dishes on the table. The cook even came out of the back where the grill was.

Randy didn't seem to require an answer because he kept looking all around the café as though there might be a hiding place he hadn't noticed before. It was clear he'd dig anyone out of that place if he saw it.

"What is it?" Lois finally asked, her voice quaking with nerves.

Randy seemed to realize where he was then. He ducked his head.

"Nothing for you to worry about." Randy's voice was soft. "I'm looking for that foster kid."

The ranchers all stood up at that, all five pairs of boots hitting the floor at the same time.

"The new foster kid or the old one?" one of the ranchers asked, his eyes going over to where Clay still sat.

"What's happened?" another rancher asked. He was halfway to Randy by the time he finished his question.

"Someone cut all the tarps on the daffodils," Randy said, his voice outraged. "At the church! Those flowers are all frozen solid now. It's a desecration."

Randy stood there, his shoulders squared with righteous indignation. Clay wanted to say something to calm the situation, but no words came. This was the kind of fury that had led to the townspeople condemning him four years ago.

Clay looked down in time to see Allie slip around Randy.

* * *

"Now, there's no need to jump to conclusions," Allie commanded as she stood in front of the ranchers. She stretched her arms over the door as though to slow down a stampede. She'd known these men all her life, and she knew they were fair-minded if they understood a situation. "It's not as bad as it seems."

"Not as bad?" Randy turned to her in loud protest.

"It could have been an accident," Allie continued in desperation. She could see by their faces that those ranchers were ready to haul Clay back to jail.

"Those tarps were deliberately cut," Randy said firmly.

Allie noticed that even Randy swung his head until he was looking squarely at Clay. Surely they could not suspect him. "Clay didn't even—"

"Of course not," one of the ranchers said. "But he's still got his nose out of joint. Admitted as much in church before he stomped out last Sunday."

"He was only trying to tell everyone what happened," Allie said. The ranchers turned to look at her now. She put a bright smile on her face in hopes that would convince them to leave Clay alone.

It didn't work that way.

"I hope you ain't sweet on him," one of the men said instead as he shook his head with a hangdog expression on his face. "He led your brother into a life of crime and almost got him killed. It's no good if you take up with him, too."

The other ranchers nodded. Allie noted they didn't even need to discuss it among themselves. They had condemned Clay once again for the past.

The whole thing was making her mad. And here Clay was with his agent, someone he wanted to impress.

"As a matter of fact," Allie said crisply, "I've been sweet on Clay West since the day I first met him."

The entire café was silent. Allie herself was dumbfounded. The words had come out of her without any thought. The ranchers just stood there with their jaws dropped and their eyes wide. Even Clay stared at her.

"I mean," she stammered. "I think we need to reconsider. I think Clay is innocent. That's all."

"Innocent of what?" one of the ranchers asked.

Allie flushed red at his words. "We all know

he didn't cut those tarps. He's a good man. We need to look elsewhere for someone to blame."

The café seemed to have grown overly hot in the time Allie stood there with the door open. Which was impossible, of course, but her neck sure did feel warm. She stepped inside and let the door close behind her.

She didn't want to look at Clay, but she did anyway. He was sitting there with a frown on his face. Not that she knew what that meant. Was he happy that she'd made a fool of herself telling everyone that she liked him? Or was he just pleased that she had finally stood up for him in this town?

A tiny doubt sneaked into her thoughts. Was she willing to declare him not guilty of that robbery years ago or was she just saying he couldn't have cut those tarps? She had nothing but emotions to guide her either way.

"It has to be the new foster kid then," Randy said, breaking the silence. "And I think he's around here somewhere. I saw that pickup he drives outside."

The ranchers started to head toward the door, and Allie stepped out of their way. Clay and Randy followed the other men outside. She had no choice but to follow, as well.

Chapter Fifteen

Clay knew what it was like to be a foster kid who was blamed for everything that happened for miles around. That teenager, Hen, probably wasn't guilty of this, and Clay couldn't stand by while a mob of angry men confronted him. If they badgered the boy, Clay didn't know what would happen.

Unfortunately, they didn't need to go far to find Hen. He was standing against the panel of the truck he drove, wearing ragged black jeans and a black parka. His legs crossed at the ankles and his arms crossed in front of him. He was the picture of defiance, right down to the dangling earring that shone in the rising sun and the lit cigarette between his lips.

"Where's your knife?" Randy demanded as he faced off with the teenager.

"What's it to you?" Hen answered back with a snarl in his voice.

"Somebody used something sharp to cut through those tarps by the church," Randy said. "It would take a knife."

"That was a dumb idea anyway," Hen said. "What kind of church worries about having flowers for Easter?"

Allie gasped but didn't say anything.

Clay felt unqualified to answer that question, although he had learned a thing or two from all his readings of the Gospel of Luke.

"The church needs your respect," Clay finally said. "You're better off to confess now if you cut those tarps."

Hen didn't look convinced, but he did move his glare from Randy to Clay.

"You're one to talk," Hen said to Clay as he flicked the ash from the end of his cigarette. "Heard you're a jailbird. Real bad guy."

Clay was glad the agent had stayed inside, although the fact that Clay had served time was not a secret.

"Look, just show us the inside of your pickup," Randy demanded. "We want to see if you have a knife on you."

Hen smirked and stepped away from the pickup. "Be my guest."

Clay watched the teenager as Randy, Allie

and the ranchers searched the vehicle. Hen stood away from them, glaring as he followed their movements. Hen was trying to look tough, but Clay thought he saw a twitch in the teenager's face.

"The pickup's clean," Randy announced when they'd finished. He looked at Hen speculatively then. "Take that coat off and let's see if it's tucked in there."

"Man, its cold out here," Hen complained, but he unzipped the parka and took it off. Randy quickly felt the seams and pockets of the coat. Then he handed it back to Hen. "It's clean."

One of the ranchers asked Hen to turn around before he put his coat back on so he could see if he had a knife hidden anywhere.

"He's clean," the rancher agreed.

The rest of the men looked defeated, but Clay wasn't convinced Hen was as innocent as he was pretending to be. The ranchers, Randy and Allie started to walk across the street to the church. Clay kept standing where he was.

When the others were far enough away that they couldn't hear, Clay leaned over to Hen. "Pull up your right pant leg."

Hen looked scared for the first time this morning. "You got no call to—"

"Pull it up," Clay repeated.

The teenager still didn't, so Clay reached down and tugged the jeans up enough that the knife's sheath was visible.

"They were just some stupid flowers," Hen said. "It wasn't like I killed anybody."

Clay was silent.

"What are you going to do?" Hen finally asked defiantly.

"I'm not going to do anything," Clay said. "You are. You're going to go over to the church and tell everyone what you did. Then you're going to apologize and ask them to forgive you. Then you're going to do everything you can to make up for what you did."

"Humph," Hen said. "Why should I do that? They didn't even see my knife."

"I saw it," Clay said. "And if you want to keep yourself out of jail, you'll do as I say."

"Like you're such an expert," Hen muttered.

Clay laughed at that. "Frankly, in this situation, I am just about as expert as you'll find. Now let's go."

He was surprised at how easily the boy went with him.

Allie almost cried when she saw the shredded tarps behind the church. Generations ago, the congregation had chosen this side of the building for the Easter sunrise service because the cemetery stood here. They wanted to share the Resurrection joy of the morning with their beloved ones who lay in this sacred ground. Allie herself always stopped to pray at her mother's grave on Easter morning.

And now the area where the daffodils had been planted looked devastated. The gravestones were damp. The air was cold. Heavy plastic was lying on top of green shoots, all pushed to the ground by what looked like tire marks.

"Look what they did!" Randy said as he used his arm to sweep the scene of destruction. "There's no way to save any of the flowers for Easter morning."

Allie looked over at the faces of the five ranchers who had followed Randy over here. They were among the churchgoers who had made the decision to hold the Easter sunrise service here years ago. Half of them had wives or children buried in this cemetery. They understood the joy of Resurrection Sunday. They knew faith held families together, and this was their one day to celebrate that fact. The daffodils were their gift to God in thanks for what He'd given them. One of the men had plowed the land last fall so it would be ready for planting. Another had come with his two grandsons to put the stakes in to hold up the tarps.

Yet another had taken care of buying the daffodil bulbs.

Now they were shocked and angry.

All of their eyes turned to look as Clay and that boy, Hen, came walking around the side of the church to where they stood.

The storm wasn't the only thing responsible for the chill that hung in the air. No one greeted the newcomers. The silence was long and tense.

Finally, Clay spoke. "Hen, here, has something to say."

The teenager swallowed. His face was pale. Allie could see he was terrified.

"It's time to tell the truth," Clay said to the boy. "It might be hard, but a man isn't much if he can't be honest. It's what makes you who you are."

Allie blinked. *Oh, my,* she thought. She suddenly understood why it was so important to Clay that people believe him when he said he didn't plan that robbery. He believed with all his heart that everything that he was demanded he be truthful.

She stared at him. He was so focused on the boy that he didn't see her, but Allie knew she needed to sit down with him later today and tell him that she believed him. She had no choice. She could see that Clay wouldn't lie. She let the knowledge sink into her heart. That meant robbing the gas station had been all Mark's doing. And Clay had been sent to prison for something he hadn't done.

She heard Hen clear his throat. "I—I'm the one who did this."

Hen held up a knife he had gotten from somewhere. "I'm guilty."

The ranchers stared at the boy, unmoved by his confession.

"But why?" one of them finally asked. "Why would you do this?"

"I—" the boy started and then stopped to look at Clay.

"Go on," Clay encouraged him. "You're not done here yet, so you may as well answer the question."

"Everyone was so perfect inside there," Hen said as he jerked his head in the direction of the church. "There's no one like me there. So I just did it. I'm sorry."

The boy's words had been raw when he spoke them, his voice low and hoarse. Allie thought he might be on the verge of tears.

She wasn't sure how the ranchers managed to communicate, but she saw them shift as one and she knew that a decision had been made.

"I've failed at more things than you can possibly know, boy," one of the ranchers said.

"I've been an alcoholic. A liar. I'm not as perfect as you might think."

"I have a terrible temper," another one offered. "Ask anyone. I do battle with myself almost every day."

"I cheated on my wife," another one said. "It was many years ago—before I became a Christian—but I thank God every day that she forgave me. I don't stack up better than any man."

"Elmer and me," one of the last two men said as nodded to the man beside him, "we've been swindled so bad we almost lost everything. One of those pyramid schemes with a buy-in that was supposed to pay off big-time. Greed, you know. That's our downfall."

Elmer nodded. "None of us are perfect in that church. We're all just forgiven. God loves us and He loves you."

Tears were streaming down the boy's face by now. Allie could see he was touched and embarrassed by his emotions.

"I'm sorry for what I did," Hen mumbled.

The ranchers nodded in unison.

"And—" Clay prompted the boy.

"And I plan to do anything I can to make things better," Hen pledged.

Allie had tears in her eyes, too. She wished the community had gathered around Clay all those years ago like they were doing with this boy. "I plan to make things better, too," Allie said as she went over and stood by Clay.

She watched him, standing there looking satisfied that Hen had confessed and been forgiven.

"You're a good man," she said to Clay, soft enough that only he could hear.

He seemed startled at her words, turning to study her.

"Everyone knows that," she added, feeling self-conscious. "Even if they haven't admitted it yet."

A slow grin spread across his face. "I'm just glad that you know it."

Allie smiled back. "Me, too."

She hadn't felt so happy in years. And then she remembered the daffodils. Easter wasn't going to be the same in Dry Creek without the daffodils.

Chapter Sixteen

Clay went out to the barn the next morning. He'd told Hen to meet him there. The day was warmer than the day before. The storm was over. There was no way to physically replace the daffodils that had been destroyed, but Clay knew they could go all out and paint the wagon with pictures of daffodils. Traditionally, the wagon carried a large cross, and Clay figured they could make a plywood backdrop to put behind the cross that would show a field of daffodils.

Clay had brought down the yellow and green paints from the hayloft and had already painted a small section of daffodils. He planned to have Hen paint the yellow and recruit Jeremy to paint the leaves.

Allie came by before Hen arrived.

Clay saw her standing just inside the barn.

She'd been quiet, and Clay wanted to take time to enjoy looking at her before she made herself known. The sun shone through the strands of her hair, giving her a coppery look. She looked nervous, but not scared. Clay refused to think of her leaving in a little over a week, but he knew she planned to go back to her job in Jackson Hole.

Clay hoped in a few months he'd be making enough money with his sketches that they could at least make plans for a future where Allie stayed on the ranch she loved. He didn't know how to even talk to her about that, though, so he just watched her from a distance.

She stepped closer and quietly cleared her throat. He looked up.

"I want you to know I believe you about that robbery," she said without any drama. "I'm sorry I held on to my anger. I think that's what stopped me from seeing that you wouldn't lie."

Clay leaned back on his heels. He had squatted down to draw some more daffodils on the front of the wagon. He had hoped for years to someday hear Allie say she believed him, but now that she was saying it, he realized how unfair he'd been.

"I'm sorry I've been pressing you to take my side," he said as he stood up. "I'm willing to compromise. We can just start from now and move forward. You don't have to believe I'm innocent."

He wiped his hands on the cloth he used to clean up any paint splatters.

He appreciated that Allie was willing to say she believed his side of the story. But hearing all of those old ranchers confess their faults to Hen yesterday made Clay wonder if he wasn't too proud of being truthful. Quite often people saw the same situation from different perspectives. He didn't need to always have everyone agree with him.

Allie frowned. "Okay."

Clay saw he'd only confused her. He stepped closer and opened his arms wide. "Come here."

Allie stepped into his arms, and he was centered. "What I'm trying to say is that I don't want anything to come between us again. Not who's guilty or innocent. Right or wrong. Rich or poor."

Allie leaned back and eyed him wryly. "Rich or poor? I'm guessing we don't have to worry about the rich side of that one."

"We'll get by," Clay said confidently. He hadn't told Allie yet that his agent was getting bids already for a series of sketches on the goat and horse. Of course, nothing was certain yet. The bids could evaporate. The truth was, he had nothing to offer Allie yet. He was a broken-down ex-con with a future that could go up in smoke.

"So we're still friends?" Allie asked hopefully.

That stopped Clay. He felt like he was on a precipice with her. But she seemed to be on firm ground. He saw now that she had spoken out to shore up what she thought of as a good friendship. She didn't look like she wanted anything more.

"Yeah, sure," Clay said.

Suddenly, Clay envied Randy his ability to buy all those slices of chiffon pie. He wished there was a similar way for him to show Allie that he wanted more than friendship.

Clay had let the moment pass, and he realized he might as well get back to the wagon. Allie had already started looking around to check on the animals.

"Wondering where the goat is?" he asked as he picked up the marker he was using to outline the floral motif on the wagon.

Allie nodded. "Remember that man Stan said we shouldn't turn our backs on him?"

"The goat only gets mad if we're working with the horses," Clay replied. "Besides, I put him in the stall over there by the pig."

Allie stayed to work with the Appaloosas. Clay knew she had a good eye for telling which two horses would work best together when harnessed to the wagon.

When Hen showed up, he went right to work. Clay was a little surprised the teenager took to the task with reasonable enthusiasm.

"Sheriff Wall talk to you?" he asked the boy after a while.

Hen nodded.

"I remember a couple of problems I had with him when I was here before," Clay remarked. "He can be a powerful motivator."

"You ain't kidding," Hen said and looked over his shoulder toward the barn door as though he was making sure the sheriff wasn't there. "He said he was going to keep an eye on me, and I'm thinking maybe he's with the Mafia or something."

"I don't think they have the Mafia around here," Clay said, trying to control his laugh.

"Well, he sure sounds like he could do something if he doesn't like what he sees," Hen said.

Clay let his laugh roll out.

"He'll get the church talking to you is what he'll do," Clay said.

Hen grinned wryly at that. "Those old men are pretty tough customers."

Clay nodded. He figured Hen had gotten the lay of the land. He would do fine as long as he was in Dry Creek. That fact gave Clay a good feeling. Maybe if things had been different when he'd been here, he would have done well, too. He had realized by now that if he and Mark had taken the church's challenge more seriously back then and had read the Gospel of Luke, they might have stayed in the bunkhouse that night talking theology instead of driving all over the country looking for more beer.

He couldn't wait to see Mark and find out what he thought about that Gospel. It sure was a fascinating account, Clay told himself. He'd read it several times by now. He didn't see how it related to him, but Mark might know.

Clay's alarm clock woke him at four o'clock on Easter morning. The night was dark. Everything was planned down to the minute, though, and he needed to get up. Allie was waking about now, too. She was going to drive to the nursing home and bring Mark back to Dry Creek. Randy and Clay were going to get the wagon and horses to the church. Mr. Nelson and Jeremy would drive in later in the old red pickup. That would be where Mark would wait until everything was set to go.

Clay was drinking a second cup of coffee when Allie knocked on the bunkhouse door.

He opened it, and she presented him with a bag from the hardware store.

"For Hen," she said as he looked inside the bag and saw the white Stetson sitting there.

"He's worked hard lately, and I thought he might like to share in the Nelson family Easter hat tradition," Allie said.

"He'll like it very much," Clay said. He should have thought of doing this himself.

"I need to be going to get Mark," Allie said. "I'll meet you at the church around six thirty."

Clay nodded and she was gone.

The barn was cold and the metal snaps on the harness colder still. Clay wrapped the leather inside his coat a bit before he put it on the two horses. Allie had chosen the stallion and the tallest of the mares to pull the wagon. Randy helped get the horses in position, and Clay draped the harnesses around them. The goat nearly started attacking until Randy showed the animal where to stand beside the stallion.

The rooster started crowing about the time Hen showed up. The teenager's hair was tousled and his eyes sleepy. He had his faded black jeans and the black parka on. But someone had found him a white cotton shirt, and the collar was crisp. For the boy, this was as dressed up as he was likely to get.

"Happy Easter morning," Clay said as he held the bag out to Hen.

"For me?" the teenager asked in disbelief.

Clay nodded and Hen opened the bag.

"Ah!" the teenager said with a triumphant shout. He took the white Stetson out of the bag and put it on his head. "I'm a regular Dry Creeker now."

Clay and Randy were both grinning, too.

"You sure are," Clay said as he stepped up to the seat on the wagon. Randy told Hen he could ride in the pickup with him. It was too dark outside still for the team to make their way down the roads, so Randy was going to drive his pickup in front of them and light the way.

Clay had stacked as many wool blankets as he could in the back of the wagon. He'd need them to keep Mark warm. The tall wooden cross that they would eventually set up in the back was waiting at the church. They would add that to the wagon later, just before they did their procession through town.

The road was bumpier behind a horse team than in a pickup. Clay discovered that as he made slow progress toward Dry Creek. Mr. Nelson had told him it would take some time, and the older man was right.

Clay rather appreciated the quiet of the

drive, though. He'd read the crucifixion account in the Gospel of Luke again last night. He could picture it better driving through the cold damp morning than lying in bed at night. He still didn't find a way to connect to the story, though. Everything seemed to have happened so long ago to people so very different from him.

They arrived at the church before the sun started to rise. That had been Clay's plan. He wanted the wagon to be a surprise to the people of Dry Creek. Hen had worked hard on painting the flowers.

Clay looked at where all of the daffodils had been planted. The plastic was cleared and the dead stalks raked up. Randy showed Clay where the cross was kept, and they both tied it into place on the back of the wagon.

They were finished with everything when Mr. Nelson drove up in the old red pickup.

"Where's Jeremy?" Clay asked as the rancher stepped out of the vehicle.

"Mrs. Hargrove offered to feed him breakfast," the older man said. "I decided there was no reason for him to sit out here in the cold when he could be eating her cinnamon rolls. Besides…" The man's voice trailed off.

Clay understood. Mark would wonder at a small boy being tended by his father. Clay didn't have much time to consider things, though, because Allie drove up in her father's SUV. Mark had his face almost pressed to the window, he looked so eager.

There was room for only one vehicle behind the church, so Mr. Nelson went to greet his son and help him move to the red pickup. Clay climbed in behind the wheel after Mark was settled in the passenger seat.

"Warm enough?" Clay asked as he adjusted the knob to the heater.

Mark nodded as he looked around the vehicle. "I just can't believe I'm here in this old pickup with you. We had some great times, didn't we?"

Mark didn't seem to need an answer to his question. He ran his hands over the dashboard and fiddled with the radio. A scratchy sound came on.

"Someone fixed the radio?" Mark asked in surprise. "I was intending to do that."

"Must have been your dad," Clay answered.

Mark frowned then. "That crack wasn't there before."

He pointed to the left side of the windshield.

Clay was becoming uncomfortable. He hadn't expected Mark to be so aware of things. How were they ever going to keep it a secret from him that he'd lost four years of his life?

Then Clay saw that Mark was looking behind him.

"What happened to my rifle?" Mark asked, frowning. "I always keep it in the rack behind us."

Clay guessed the rifle was buried in the sheriff's department somewhere as evidence of the armed robbery. Or did the authorities return those items to Mr. Nelson? Clay had no clue. He could not even think of a plausible thing to say to Mark that was the truth.

"We're going to need to get out there on the wagon," Clay said instead as his hand reached for the door handle.

Allie walked with them over to the wagon. She hadn't intended to go, but Clay realized he might need help. He hoped Mark would forget about his missing rifle, but he had a feeling his friend was thinking about something.

"Come with us," he mouthed to Allie.

Clay and Allie set Mark between them on the wagon seat. He was wrapped in a half-dozen blankets, and his face was glowing with excitement. Hen stepped into the back of the wagon, behind the painted plywood. He was to keep that and the cross steady.

"We're doing it," Mark leaned over and said to Clay.

Clay nodded.

"I've been praying for this day ever since I started reading the Gospel of Luke again," Mark said. "I believe it all."

Clay was silent. Finally, he said, "It's a compelling story. But it happened so long ago."

Mark snorted. "It could have happened yesterday. Jesus comes down to earth. Everything goes crazy. Then a bunch of people get together and convict an innocent man—"

The words hit Clay like a bullet. All of the pieces fell into place. He'd never considered it that way. If anyone understood what had happened to him, it was Jesus. He might have lived thousands of years ago, but he knew what it was like to be innocent and have everyone look at him like he was guilty.

"We need to pull out," Mr. Nelson called, and Clay picked up the reins.

The sun was starting to rise by the time Clay got the wagon to the start mark outside the small town. Almost a hundred people were huddled together at the stop sign that marked the beginning of the procession.

Clay heard a collective gasp of delight when he pulled the wagon close enough for people to see all the flowers painted on the sides.

"Hallelujah!" someone shouted. "We have our daffodils."

"Praise God," another said.

Clay figured it was a happy group that fell into step behind the wagon. He drove slowly. The goat did his job, guiding the stallion as they moved forward.

Prayer started to bubble up inside Clay as he drove.

"I think Jesus knows me," he whispered to Mark as they rolled along.

Mark squeezed his hand. "He does."

"I heard that," Allie chimed in quietly from where she sat. "I'm so glad you realize that."

"Sometimes it takes me a while," Clay said as he glanced back at the tall cross standing there. He knew without thinking about it that he was never going to be the same.

"Some things take me some time, too," Mark said quietly.

Clay didn't say anything.

"That rifle—" Mark started and looked over at Clay. "Did that night happen? Did I leave you pumping gas and take that rifle into that gas station?"

The people walking behind them had started to sing a hymn, and the words wrapped around Clay with comfort.

"We can talk about it later," Clay said. "Don't strain to remember."

He didn't know how Mark would feel

when he realized the enormity of what they had done.

Clay pulled the wagon into place behind the church, and everyone sitting there climbed down. Allie helped Mark into the shelter of the red pickup. By now, the sun had turned golden as it rose in the east. The stones in the cemetery were bathed in light, and Clay saw others looking to the graveyard, as well.

Allie walked over and stood beside him as he eyed the small crosses on the burial ground. The hymnal being sung changed, and Clay heard words about Jesus conquering death. He understood now why the people of Dry Creek celebrated Easter morning with as much joy as they could muster and why they did so in the presence of their departed loved ones.

Clay listened to the pastor's Easter sermon, the peace inside him growing.

When the service was over and everyone else had gone inside to have coffee, Clay stood with Allie back by the wagon. He could see in her eyes that she had questions for him.

"I need some time," he told her. "I'm not the man today that I will be in a few weeks. I plan to talk with the pastor and get my life on track with God. I'm not going to ask you to wait for me, but when you come back next time from Jackson Hole, I want to talk to you about the future."

Allie looked at him soberly. "The future or our future?"

"Ours," he said. "I hope."

"I don't need to wait," she said softly.

"Oh." That didn't sound promising to Clay. "I wanted to have a chance to show you I can be better. You deserve a good husband and…"

He didn't know what else to say. Life didn't always give second chances. He looked down at Allie and stood silent. He'd endured loneliness for most of his life. He could handle it again.

Allie looked up at him. She'd dreamed about Clay for over four years. When she'd known him earlier her feelings had been more a teenage crush than anything. Getting to know him now, though, she could see the solid foundation of his character. He was a good man. He was her man.

"The answer is already yes," Allie whispered. "If you need time to think about it, that's fine, but don't expect me to change my mind."

Allie watched the sun rise again in Clay's eyes. He reached up and traced her cheek with an expression of wonder on his face.

"I never thought," he murmured.

She reached her own hand up to touch his cheek.

"I love you," he said simply.

Allie knew he did. Clay never lied.

"You're going to make me cry," she said.

"That won't do," Clay said with a smile as he dipped his head toward her.

The kiss was her undoing. A flash of sweet promise sizzled through her as his lips explored her.

"I love you, too," she said.

It wasn't until they parted that they noticed half the people in the church were watching them from the building's back window.

"Oh, oh," she said.

Clay gripped her shoulder in support.

Then she saw the people act in unison, all giving her an exuberant thumbs-up signal.

"I think that's your welcome home." She smiled as she turned to Clay.

She knew then that, as long as she lived, she would never forget the look of wonder on Clay's face.

Epilogue

In June of that same year

Sunshine streamed in through the side windows, but Allie stood in the shadows at the back of the Dry Creek church. She clutched a bouquet of pink roses in one hand and held her father's arm with the other. She hoped no one could see how nervous she was. All she could do was stare ahead at Clay as he stood in the charcoal-gray suit he'd bought especially for today. He was hundreds of feet away, but she could feel his gaze warming her. Suddenly, she was calm.

She and Clay had wanted a simple wedding, but the women of the church asked to be part of the celebration, and now everything shone. Rose bouquets lined the aisle and gave a sweet scent to the air. Two of the town's best seamstresses had made Allie's white silk dress. Another had made a short veil for her head. Every pew was filled with neighbors and friends, all of them attired in their Sunday-best clothes.

Allie and Clay had finished their marriage counseling with the pastor weeks ago, and he had pronounced them a good match. Now he looked over at Clay with approval and nodded.

That was the signal for Doris June Hargrove to stand and walk up to the piano.

Allie took a deep breath and turned.

"It's almost time," she whispered to her father.

He nodded before glancing back at the church door furtively.

"They're not coming," Allie said.

Everyone had thought her brother's old girlfriend, Hannah, would relent and allow Allie's nephew to attend the wedding.

"She's got to talk to Mark eventually," her father muttered.

"Hannah says not," Allie countered. A curt note had come from a lawyer last week; Hannah had been informed of the change in Mark's condition and he had tried to contact her, asking to meet his son, but she never answered any of Mark's messages.

Allie didn't know what to do. Mark had regained his memory and told all of the people in Dry Creek what had really happened the night of the robbery. He knew Jeremy was his son. But Hannah kept refusing to see him or to let him see Jeremy.

Allie told herself there was nothing she could do about it today.

The music to the wedding march started. Allie and her father began to walk forward.

From then on, Allie couldn't think of anyone but Clay. His voice when he spoke his vows made her shiver. She couldn't believe she had wanted to send this man away when he appeared back at the ranch in March.

When Clay finished his vows, he added something they hadn't rehearsed.

"Allie Nelson, I will love you until the day I die," he said with such sincerity that Allie heard a flutter of sighs in the pews behind her.

"And I will love you," Allie said, blinking back tears.

Clay kissed her then, fierce and hard like he was sealing a bargain.

The pastor cleared his throat indulgently. "We're not quite to that part of the ceremony yet."

A ripple of soft chuckles came from the pews.

"We don't mind doing it twice," Clay said with a grin.

Allie said her vows, her voice not wavering once.

"And now," the pastor said, "I pronounce you man and wife." He turned to Clay. "You can now officially kiss your bride."

Allie felt the warmth of that kiss right down to her toes. She was happy and knew Clay was, too.

* * * * *

*If you liked this story,
pick up these other heartwarming books
from Janet Tronstad:*

*SLEIGH BELLS FOR DRY CREEK
LILAC WEDDING IN DRY CREEK
WILDFLOWER BRIDE IN DRY CREEK
SECOND CHANCE IN DRY CREEK
WHITE CHRISTMAS IN DRY CREEK
ALASKAN SWEETHEARTS*

Available now from Love Inspired!

*Find more great reads at
www.LoveInspired.com*

Dear Reader,

I know from the emails you (my readers) send that many of us go through periods of discouragement, especially during the winter months. Life sometimes seems a little harder when the ground is cold. But when those first signs of spring appear, everything is better. Grass starts to grow. New buds appear. Hope comes alive. I tried to capture that feeling of new life in my *Easter for Dry Creek*. The book starts with a freezing late-winter snow and a family in need of healing.

If this past winter has been hard for you, I pray my book points you to a time of reflection on the new life God gives us anytime we ask, but especially at Easter. If you do find the book helpful in that regard, please email me through my website at www.JanetTronstad. com. Just click where it says to contact me. I love to hear from my readers.

In the meantime, may your spring be enriched in many ways with new hope in God's love and a deepening connection to nature's beauty. I am blessed because, in my new home in central California, I enjoy a dozen rosebushes that sit right outside my patio. The red, pink and yellow flowers cheer my heart every morning when I see them.

Again, I hope you will drop me a note through my website. Until then, may God bless you and yours.

Sincerely yours,

Janet Tronstad

Get 2 Free Books,
Plus 2 Free Gifts—
just for trying the Reader Service!

LIS17R

Get 2 Free Books,
Plus 2 Free Gifts—
just for trying the Reader Service!

HOMETOWN HEARTS ♥

YES! Please send me **The Hometown Hearts Collection** in Larger Print. This collection begins with 3 FREE books and 2 FREE gifts in the first shipment. Along with my 3 free books, I'll also get the next 4 books from the Hometown Hearts Collection, in LARGER PRINT, which I may either return and owe nothing, or keep for the low price of $4.99 U.S./ $5.89 CDN each plus $2.99 for shipping and handling per shipment*. If I decide to continue, about once a month for 8 months I will get 6 or 7 more books, but will only need to pay for 4. That means 2 or 3 books in every shipment will be FREE! If I decide to keep the entire collection, I'll have paid for only 32 books because 19 books are FREE! I understand that accepting the 3 free books and gifts places me under no obligation to buy anything. I can always return a shipment and cancel at any time. My free books and gifts are mine to keep no matter what I decide.

262 HCN 3432 462 HCN 3432

Name (PLEASE PRINT)

Address   Apt. #

City   State/Prov.   Zip/Postal Code

Signature (if under 18, a parent or guardian must sign)

Mail to the **Reader Service:**

IN U.S.A.: P.O. Box 1867, Buffalo, NY. 14240-1867
IN CANADA: P.O. Box 609, Fort Erie, Ontario L2A 5X3

* Terms and prices subject to change without notice. Prices do not include applicable taxes. Sales tax applicable in NY. Canadian residents will be charged applicable taxes. This offer is limited to one order per household. All orders subject to approval. Credit or debit balances in a customer's account(s) may be offset by any other outstanding balance owed by or to the customer. Please allow 4 to 6 weeks for delivery. Offer available while quantities last. Offer not available to Quebec residents.

READERSERVICE.COM

Manage your account online!

- Review your order history
- Manage your payments
- Update your address

> ### We've designed the Reader Service website just for you.

Enjoy all the features!

- Discover new series available to you, and read excerpts from any series.
- Respond to mailings and special monthly offers.
- Browse the Bonus Bucks catalog and online-only exculsives.
- Share your feedback.

Visit us at:

ReaderService.com

RS16R